THE DESIGNER
STRONG WOMEN
BOOK 3

TESS MOLESWORTH

Published by Tess Molesworth

tessmolesworth@gmail.com

First published 2025

Text © Tess Molesworth 2025

The moral right of Tess Molesworth to be identified as the author of this work has been asserted.

All rights reserved.

Without limiting the rights under copyright reserved above, no part of this publication may be reproduced, stored in or introduced into a retrieval system, or transmitted, in any form or by any means, without the prior written permission of both the copyright owner and the publisher of this book.

For any copyright queries, please email Tess Molesworth at tessmolesworth@gmail.com

This is a work of fiction. Names, characters, places, and incidents are either the product of the author's imagination or are used fictitiously, and any resemblance to actual persons, living or dead, business establishments, events or locales is entirely coincidental.

 A catalogue record for this book is available from the National Library of Australia.

ISBN 9781763584648 (Print)

ISBN 9781763584655 (eBook)

Editorial by Stephanie Cuthbert

Cover Art & Formatting by DAZED Designs

Printed by IngramSpark

We're all strong enough to achieve what others think we can't. Prove them wrong with a smile.

CHAPTER 1
LEXI

Every day this week I've been up before dawn. Often the birds are not even making a noise. For me, it's the most peaceful and fulfilling time to open the gym and get a workout done.

I own a women's only gym in our postcard perfect seaside town. Most people come for the sunsets or summer festivals. I grew up here, away from the hustle and bustle of the big cities dotted along the west coast. It only seemed right to give back to the community and offer a service for women.

This morning is no different to the others this week, two classes before seven, then home to have a post-workout meal, shower, change of clothes and I'm back in the office by nine. It's Friday, so there's another class at ten for new mothers before a day of planning and accountability check-in messages with my clients and members.

My gym is open until five this afternoon for members, no one – not even the diehards want to train after five on a Friday.

Finally sitting down at my desk after the mother's group

to do my planning for the next twelve week block, an email alert chimes.

To: *lexi.monelli@freakfitness.com*

From: *garry.cawbourne@mayor.com*

Subject: *Meeting*

To Lexi,
Please be at my office at 11:30am regarding an issue with your gym.

Quickly looking at the time, I see it's quarter past eleven. That slimy bastard knows my class schedule and sent this email to ensure I have hardly any time to prepare for whatever bullshit his office is trying to hold against me.

Please present yourself at the front desk of the council offices before 11:30 to ensure you can attend the meeting in a prompt manner.

Yours sincerely,

Mayor Garry Cawbourne.

Not even bothering to shut the computer down properly, I race from my office, pulling the door locked and closing the front door of the gym as well. If there are any deities, I'll make it to the council office with time to spare.

Checking my phone as I'm racing up the steps outside the council chambers, I've got three minutes to spare as I reach the front desk.

Bea raises her head from her phone and holds my eyes while I catch my little breath from running outside. No one likes running up steps, no matter how fit you are. "Here for meeting with Garry," I say, ensuring my heart rate is back to a normal pace before I face the man who oversees my beloved town.

She rises from her desk behind the main counter to come and direct me to the meeting room. A little distance from me, her eyes are imploring for me to read the message hidden there. I wish I could, but I am still trying to work out what and why this is happening. She was in my five-am class and between the jokes, swearing and sweating achievements from the class, she didn't mention anything about this meeting.

"This way Lexi." She moves to a door which leads back to where other offices and the conference rooms are housed. As I pass through, she whispers from the side of her mouth. "I didn't know. I'm on your side." If there are security cameras at this point, they wouldn't pick up sound or movement from her lips.

No expression or acknowledgement can be seen on my face as I follow her down to the conference room. It's hard to believe her. She's only been in town for about eighteen months. She doesn't know Garry like I do. He can manipulate you into a false sense of security.

As we draw nearer, I can see Garry Cawbourne focusing on his watch like he's counting down the seconds, hoping I'd be late.

I've no idea how this man became the mayor. Probably his family connections. Frankly, I paid the fine. I wasn't going to vote for him or the other candidates.

As the seconds count down on his watch, his smile grows, until he notices me standing in the doorway. "So, you made it on time."

All I do is nod. Fuck this prick. I'm not wasting oxygen on him.

"Well, I didn't expect you to be here." I can't believe him. He's just admitted he didn't actually want me here. Now I'm more thankful I busted my arse to get to this meeting.

"I'm giving you six weeks to vacate your business space. I need it for rezoning."

"What! Garry, you can't be serious?"

"It's Mayor Cawbourne."

"Really? You want me to address you as Mayor? This is ridiculous and wrong. What is this really about?"

"I have an investor who wants a main street shop frontage for his business and your area is the best description for what he wants. It's not personal, it's just business." He steeples his hands in front of his lips. I now know the true nature of this attack. Not personal, my arse. Since I was twenty-one, he has only known personal.

Noticing Bea is still in the corner watching all of this unfolding, I ensure I'm the professional person here. Regardless of the man sitting behind the desk, I will be the bigger person and not rant like a deranged woman. "Six weeks you say?" Taking the anger out of my voice, I replace it with strength. "Thank you for the information in a timely manner. Enjoy the rest of your Friday and weekend ahead."

If cartoon eyes and expressions were real, his shock of my changed demeanour would be hilarious. Bulging eyes, unhinged jaw. If I could take a photo I would. Or I could just wait until I win this battle. He won't kick me from my building or close my gym like he has wanted to do since I started. I've busted my arse for years to own my business.

When Bea and I are at the security door, waiting to get back into the front area, she says, "lunch at one in the park." Not a question, but a statement that ensures I accept the invitation.

With a flip of the switch, Bea is back to being the bubbly receptionist, like the personality I get at the gym, no matter the time of day. "Seriously Lex, that workout this morning was brutal. Where did you find that torture regimen?"

Smiling big enough so it reaches my eyes, even if my mind is going a million miles a minute with the information drop Garry just piled on me. "I have my google sources and my military connections." I tap the side of my nose for extra measures of secrecy.

"It hurts to blink."

"That's the sign of an effective workout."

Leaning forward to whisper, she adds, "If I can't sit to shit this weekend, you're getting a phone call."

I laugh. "I'll keep my phone close by just in case." I leave shaking my head and with a smile on my face that certainly wasn't there when I climbed the steps earlier.

Bea is always good at easing the mood. I appreciate it, until I'm back at my desk in the office staring at the calendar thinking about my members. Trying to understand Garry's decision. Needing to call my solicitor.

May as well start with the most pressing and easiest option of difficulty. The solicitor: Maggie Stirling.

Maggie and I went to school together and although she left to obtain her law degree, she wanted to come back stating that every town needed a solicitor, and it may as well be in the town she knew best.

I call her office, even though I have her mobile number. This has to be professional. Her receptionist puts me straight through.

"Well Lexi-Belle do you need a lunch date? Why else would you be calling me in the middle of the day?"

Now I'm back in my office, I feel I can be real. Besides

this is Maggie, she actually knows all my secrets. "Mags." There's a lump in my throat I can't seem to pass. Swallowing deeply, I try again. "Mags, Garry is kicking me out. He gave me six weeks' notice."

"The fuck he is." I smile. I know my beautiful, passionate friend has just sat up higher in her chair readying herself for war. "Give me the details."

For the next while I pass over the information and exchanges since I received the email.

"Bea is having lunch with me in the park at one. You coming?"

"Yep, count me in. Read me exactly what's on the email information for me to see if you can forward it to me or if it is secure."

Doing what she asks, we discover it could be traced. However, taking a photo, I send that to her mobile.

"Right, leave it with me. I'll meet you and Bea at one. That creep is not touching Fitness Freaks or you. See you soon."

We hang up and not for the first time I'm glad she's on my side. Maggie Stirling, in full solicitor mode is not someone you want to mess with.

Burying myself in gym session planning and accountability messages, it's easy to get lost to time. It's not until a text message comes through that I'm shocked at how easily I got carried away.

> **BEA**
> We're at the park. Got you a chicken chili wrap

> **ME**
> Shit sorry. I'm leaving now.

Grabbing my things, I'm grateful I'd rung Mags and could concentrate on what brings me happiness. However, stepping from my sanctuary, reality is coming from all angles as there seems to be more visitors than locals and it feels like anyone of them is the one in Garry's pocket wanting my building.

Quickly making my way to the park, I decide to drive even though it's only two blocks away. I need all my personal comforts at this point. At least until the initial shock of this morning's meeting is tipped more to my favour.

Seeing Mags and Bea at a picnic table in the shade adds both some privacy and relief from the late spring heat. If this is the start of the warmer weather to come, this summer will be a scorcher.

"Sorry I'm late, the blinkers were on, I just got stuck into it all." I plop down next to Mags as Bea hands me my wrap.

"It's all good," Bea says, looking down at her sandwich. "Shit Lex, I didn't know. I don't know what his deal is." She turns to Maggie. "If there's anything I can do let me know."

We make light conversations while finishing our lunch, and we're sipping our variety of refreshments when Maggie starts back on the real reason the three of us are half-hiding in a park on a Friday lunchtime.

"So, there has been nothing filed in public records about any of this. Whatever he is cooking, it hasn't been done legally, at this stage. And he's got some pretty good lawyers in his pocket and family as well."

"That's what I'm worried about. Yes, I live comfortably within my means, but I haven't got his wealth and stature."

"If nothing is public, then anything I can get from his office wouldn't be worth a piece of shit." The struggle and pain is written on Bea's face.

"This is true, but any information we can get our hands on can give us knowledge. And knowledge equals' power." Glancing at her watch Maggie adds, "Bea, if possible, I want you to snoop, dig, discover anything you can in relationship to Lex and Fitness Freaks. Lex, I want you to play nice and go about your business and leave the rest to me." Putting her sunglasses back on, Maggie stands at the end of the table. "Don't worry Lexi-Belle, I've never let you down and I'm not about to start. I'll be in touch." She air kisses us both and strides off— the most dangerous female solicitor when she's on a mission.

Bea shakes her head as if to remove those bad vibes before turning back to me in her full spirited self. "So, you ready for tonight?" She's organsied a celebration with the ladies from the gym for everyone's personal achievements with the latest program.

Her phone goes off with a text which increases the ever-present smile she wears when we're not in serious mode. When she looks up, I know she can see the uncertainty on my face. "Nope, you are not pulling out."

"Bea, I just don't think I can. I was all keen, but now after Garry, I don't think I could even fake it."

"Fuck that. You're coming out no matter what. Go home. Have a soak in the tub, put some make-up on and rock it out with the best of us. It's because of you that we can even do this."

My smile is tight and I'm not sure which way it wants to go. Full face and real at Bea's ability to make everything good. Or full face and fake but convincing. That's the easiest for me. I've perfected it over my life. Maggie is the only person who can differ between the two.

"Fine. I'll go do a couple more hours in the office and then meet you at the pub." Completely fake smile. But Bea is right, I do love celebrating the wins from the ladies and all their hard work at my gym.

Her phone chimes again and I know that's a long-lasting form of happiness showing on her face. Whoever it is they must be important. I've never seen a reaction like that to a few text messages. "I've got to go. I'll see you tonight."

Raising from the table, she's striding back to her car with her phone in hand, head down and texting not caring if people have to get out of her way.

I sit for a little longer just taking in all the aspects of the park. Getting my thoughts in order, I know I'm ready when my thoughts return to the accountability messages I have to send. I start heading back to my office and the easiest part of my job; checking in on women and identifying ways I can help them achieve their goals.

CHAPTER 2
MARCUS

It's only the second time I've arrived at my newly acquired building for my printing business, and it has all the feelings of home and roots.

Since I first walked through the doors several months ago, a lot has changed, bringing out more of the old-world charm that I knew was hidden under the layers of paint, wallpaper and additional 80's features. I contacted Flynn at Make-It-Able Construction about eight months ago and although he said six months, it was a flexible timeframe. He was able to restore the 19th century printing shop on Main Street to its original charm. Natural polish wood flooring and paneling that will never go out of style if it's decorated to suit the era welcomes me when the overhead bell chimes. It even smells like a heritage building with the scent of wood wax.

All my modern technology printing equipment is hidden behind half-wall paneling beyond the counter. Out front are pictures of previous printing memorabilia, a few of my own pieces, and the pricing board hangs over the saloon doors leading to the back.

An incoming message alert brings me back to the moment, looking down the smile is instant.

> **BEA**
>
> I know you're in town, I've seen Misty. Meet me at the pub tonight. 7pm. Be there or we are not BFF's.

Bloody Bea. That woman is the most demanding, controlling and caring person in the world. Having her in high school and every day since means I couldn't live without her. The trials and tribulations of our past is the main reason why I moved to a sleepy seaside village to plant roots on home soil and start a more permanent printing business.

> **ME**
>
> Can't make it. Misty needs a polish.

Smiling as I press send on the message, I know she'll be shaking her head and swearing under her breath with a smile encompassing her whole face.

Misty is my night mist blue 1966 mustang convertible. Bea came with me to my grandfather's will reading, letting the world know that I'd be the second owner of the highly sought after vehicle. The proviso was that I had to graduate from college in my chosen field, not what my parents wanted me to do. The magnificently prestige car is the most sought-after possession south of the Canadian border. And it wasn't until I was given the keys after graduation two years that it really sank in. My real family couldn't be there, but Bea, my chosen family, was sitting next to me in the lawyer's office when the keys were handed over.

The timing of Bea's reply brings another welcome smile to my already happy face.

> **BEA**
> Misty is more polished than a hooker's fingernails. See you at 7pm, jerk.

It's never dull with that brilliant fireball and she's one that you could never really say no to without a genuine reason. Another example why she is loved by all that cross her path.

I go back out to Misty, retrieve a box from the back seat and carry it through to the bench, ready for the business to open on Monday. I already have several online orders to fill, so it doesn't matter if there are no walk-in jobs. My website always keeps me busy.

It's Friday lunchtime and although I shouldn't fire up the machines, I can't help it. This truly is my dream job. Printing, designing, making eye-catching displays, it's quite rewarding and fulfilling. Since graduating I've been travelling and creating posters that have been compared to the great Alphonse Mucha. Europe welcomed my innovative design of popping colour and hidden designs, that I've got enough orders and recommendations to see me through the next few months.

I needed a base here in the States and when Bea suggested this seaside township and building, I couldn't resist. Being out of the city and knowing that all I need is a good internet connection for my orders and access to a post office for shipment, it wasn't hard to settle in the quaint little vintage printing building on the main street.

I arrive at the pub with less than five minutes before seven.

I've learnt that I can never be one minute late or Bea will tan my hide publicly. She's done it before.

It seems that the sleepy seaside village has found a lot more occupants than I've seen since arriving. There's a band setting up in the corner, and it's not hard to find the curvy woman with her loud, energetic happy sounds. Bea's laughter can fill any space.

It's nothing unusual to see her the centre of attention, but it's normally in mixed company, not all females.

My heart all but freezes in my chest as I make my way toward her. She knows I shut down tighter than a clam in danger on the ocean floor around that many women. But if I don't speak to her, she'll make it a million times worse.

Building more courage with every step, I get close enough to let our call for each other to be heard. The high piercing whistle has everyone stopping and looking my way. One of these bloody days we'll just walk up and tap each other on the shoulder.

Her smile is blinding, and I brace myself for the barrel of love running my way. Throwing her arms around my shoulders, I nearly have to bend in half to stop her from jumping up and locking her legs around me. We tried that once and it was not pretty for either of us. Funny has fuck, but not a sight.

"Sticks, I knew you'd come."

"Stones, you wouldn't have let me miss it."

Our nicknames for each other reflect both our personalities and physicality. Me, tall, lean, floaty, arty. Bea, curvy, strong, resilient, blunt. But when you get to know this woman, you've got someone in your corner for life.

Bea, in true fashion, quickly introduces everyone in the group and leaves me to fend for myself while she goes to the bar for our drinks.

I quickly discover that these women come from all different walks of life, but the same gym, and are just happy to be out on the town celebrating all their differences. That's the thing with Bea, she certainly makes everyone feel welcome and comfortable in themselves.

I talk with a single mum, Sarah, who although she loves her child, cherishes and is thankful for these little get togethers. A fruit tingle is placed in front of me with a straw, along with three tequila shots on the table.

Spinning fast enough to reverse time, Bea is standing there mirroring me with three shots on a tray and a devilish glint in her eyes.

"Sticks, it's been three months since we've seen each other with no real explanation. Text messages are not a point of contact, and you know it. Now don't bitch and pick 'em up."

Fuck! I hate this tradition we started long before either of us were legally allowed to drink. If we didn't catch up within the month, either face-to-face or a video call, when we got together next that's how many shots we had to have to start the night. Many liquors have passed through this deal, and it seems tonight Bea feels like tequila.

I know I can't leave her waiting or talk my way out of this deal, especially with all the female eyes pointed straight at me. There's a silence that's engulfed the bar which wasn't there before. I guess being locked in meetings and designing various famous advertisements and personal collages in Europe doesn't count as no real explanation. Time difference had never stopped us before. So here I am with three tequila shots and a very excited best friend.

Turning back, I gather the three shot glasses and place them on the tray Bea is holding in between us. This evening is starting off with a bang. My beaming smile is radiating towards my best friend. "Alright Stones, a deal's a deal. Tip 'em back."

Clinking our first drinks we throw the shots back one after the other with hardly any wincing from the burn of the liquor making its way to my stomach and spreading warmth to all other areas.

Releasing a laugh and embracing each other like the best friends we are, we turn back to the group of ladies and chat like nothing happened.

Standing around the table, I'm sipping my fruit tingle listening to Sarah and a few other women discuss their children when the most beautiful "hey, hey" comes across the table at the same time my eyes are trying to find the source.

My gaze lands on the newcomer. My ears are ringing from the chorus of screams and responses to her introduction. And I take my fill.

Standing directly across from me with one arm slung across Bea's shoulders is a breathtaking beauty. There are no other words. Shoulder length blonde hair, brown eyes, a megawatt smile and strength hidden behind life's curves. I can see muscle definition in her exposed shoulders and upper arms, a strength that comes from personal discipline and hard work, yet she still knows the value of life and living your best life.

I'm completely frozen. I've never had this instant reaction to a woman before in my life. Models in Europe: nope. Actresses in LA: nothing. College girls: zero. At twenty-four, you'd think I should have had something. Yet two words from this woman and a basic function, like breathing has ceased to operate.

Bea notices me frozen like any statue in history and just smiles at me. Yeah, not much escapes my best friend. She bends toward the mysterious beauty's ear, I'm still staring, wondering what on earth she is saying to her. I've no idea what my best friend says, but the mysterious woman's eyes automatically find mine and lock in. With a slight head tilt, every blood vessel is banging a drum around my body where her eyes take in all she can see above the table. Her smile is slow, but eventually her whole face is glowing as she finally rests on my face.

Her gaze breaks from mine and focuses on the women around the table. I can finally take a much needed sip of the bloody fruit tingle through a straw. I mean what male actually drinks from a straw? Bea knows I hate it and only did it to piss me off. Swallowing and breathing are becoming more natural as I finish off my drink. Ice clinking in my glass, I excuse myself from the group and make my way to the bar. I have no intention of wiping myself out, so a bottle of beer is enough to keep the buzz from the tequila shots and fruit tingle. I keep my back to the group of women and work on getting my shit together from just looking at her. Besides, my lust-filled brain is not ready to put my body through all that just to look at her again.

CHAPTER 3
LEXI

It took all my energy and courage to actually walk through the doors and up to the group of ladies at the pub tonight. After the bomb that Garry dropped earlier today and not hearing anything from Maggie this afternoon, it was either my favourite pyjamas, ice cream, and a movie, or the women from my gym. The women won.

Even if women are their own worst critics, and I hear every negative thing they have to say about their bodies daily. *My legs are too big. I wobble too much. I haven't got enough muscle. I want a smaller, flatter stomach.* At times all I can think is 'Fuck, just stop. You're on this side of the dirt, be thankful for that and look at what you've achieved.' It can be quite tiresome.

At thirty-six, I've fought all the internal demons most of the women in my gym have. For half of my life, I've been working in the fitness sector, and I've learnt how to wear a mask and give them the support in whatever capacity they need.

I messaged Bea earlier saying I was going to be late. Her

reply was a love heart. Guess that means she's still happy that I'm coming out.

By the time I arrived I wasn't surprised to see most of the gym ladies throwing back drinks. Their smiles were the other reason I came out. I wanted to see them in a non-confrontational setting or at least not in the gym where they indirectly compare each other without seeing their individual worth.

And they're all beautiful women. Every curve, muscle, 'wobble' and smile has a story and is well earned. This right here is one of the reasons I love my job. The joy of being an individual in a group and loving life. I know all too well the length of life and just how short it can be.

Ensuring I have my biggest, warmest welcoming smile I arrive at our table and throw my arms around Bea and one of the girls saying, 'hey, hey' in my most animated voice.

Bea is standing next to me, tucked under one arm while my smile just grows with the cheers of welcome and celebration in all that we are.

I'm chatting with Patty about her weekend plans, when Bea whispers in my ear, "Don't look now, but my best friend is locked frozen on you from across the table."

In what I hope is my best description of bedroom eyes, I drag my gaze over every inch of the only man in the group.

I did think it was weird a man was in a group of women from a ladies only gym, but I won't judge and now I know why.

He's dressed better than any other male in the pub. In a tight sweater highlighting biceps and my imagination. I've no idea what's below the height on the table. The sharp angles accentuate his features ensures that with each pass of my gaze, I'm loving the potential of a great time.

From the corner of my eye, I watch him make his way to

the bar and wait there with his back to our group. Gathering all my strength, I excuse myself saying, "it's not a celebration unless we're all drinking".

Stopping next to him, I'm leaning on the bar close enough that I can feel his body heat raising the hair on my arm, but still feeling as though I've got to cross a canyon to reach him.

"I'm Lexi, and you are?" It seems weird that I've got to introduce myself first, but in my line of work, personality is the majority of the job. And it takes all my effort to not reach out and trace all the tight angles being highlighted under his tight sweater and jeans.

His actions are timed and I'm worried I've scared him away already. Then his torso is facing me, and his eyes are darting all over my face trying to capture and memorise every feature. "I'm Marcus, Bea's best friend."

I'm not sure why he needed to add that little bit of information, but it's noted. She had mentioned her best friend was moving to town. I thought it would be a female and another membership. Does this mean he's single?

It's the start of the summer season— my time to shine. Although, if he's Bea's best friend, he's likely her age and younger men are not my regular flavour. Normally I like my one-night stands about my age. My body is starting to buzz just being in his presence. It's an unusual feeling with his age, but I'm not going to ignore my body's response to him. Getting to know him and seeing where it goes can't be the worst thing for the evening.

"How do you know Bea?" His question snaps me from my inner monologue. Fuck, ten words from this man and I'm beginning to question my standards. His voice has a touch of velvet to it and my body is responding more than I want to admit.

"I'm the owner of Fitness Freaks, a ladies only gym. What brings you to town?"

"I've just moved here and started my printing business."

He pulls out a business card from his wallet showing the design: PRIperfectNT, with a confetti background as the design.

Thank God I haven't had anything to drink because I'm not too sure if I'd get the cryptic name of his business correct.

My quizzical study of his business card has him lifting the corner of his mouth. Hesitantly I say, "Perfect in print?"

It's a question, but I know instantly I'm correct and his smile says it all. "You've got it. Sometimes I want to see if I've made a mistake designing my business cards like this."

Grabbing our drinks we make our way back toward the rowdy women letting their hair down. And rightly so. I love seeing them like this. No evidence of their personal demons hunting their inner thoughts.

The night moves through drinks flowing, laughs louder than the music and hips swaying. Often, I catch Marcus smiling and staring at me. He's polite and caring to all the ladies but there's a hidden glint in his eyes when he's glancing my way.

Bea is in fine form, like when she's in the gym. A social force to be reckoned with. As our group becomes smaller, we seem to get louder and more energetic on the dance floor. It's hard to stop when everything the band plays is swinging through your hips.

A favourite song of mine comes on and I can't help myself, I grab Marcus and pull him onto the dance floor amongst the other dancers. It's a song that requires a partner with hips to sway and hands to hold you close. It's probably the alcohol taking over, but all night I've been eyeing this new man in town. Normally anyone staying longer than the season only results in a big NO! But there is something about him lighting a spark moving around my body.

Our bodies are entwined, and I can feel every part meshing together. He's not built like a gym junkie, but there's something keeping him lean with sharp angles and muscles in all the right places.

Spinning around, so my back is to his front, raising my hands, to hold behind his head, I can feel every glorious plane of his body against mine. He caresses across my midsection, never going lower or higher. His thumb brushes the underside of my breast through my shirt and the feeling has me swaying more into his touch. I want him. I want the indecent. The raw hunger a warm-blooded man offers any sexy woman.

Grabbing his hands off my stomach, I place them directly on my hips under my shirt. Flesh on flesh. His touch is warm, but it feels more than the heat from dancing. This feels like every bad decision rolled into the right man.

"You keep swaying that arse across my cock and everyone will see what I want." His deep sensual voice registers in my ear and I feel the difference in his pants.

The song switch happens seamlessly and although the tempo is different, I can't stop grinding my arse along his front. His hands haven't stopped their exploration of my waistline, and fire is coursing my system in the wake of his touches. My nipples are pebbling under my bra and I swear if he slips his hand down the front of my skirt, he'd find me wet. Drenched. Within two songs, my body has never felt so alive.

I haven't felt like this for a fucking long time. Yes, I've hooked up, mainly with summer flings that come here for the festivals, but this feels different.

Spinning back so I can look up into his eyes I lean up to reach his ear. "What are you going to do about that rod in your pants?"

Leaning down, he lightly breathes up the side of my neck leaving goosebumps as his breath cools my dance sweaty skin. "Not what you think. But it'll be what you want."

Breaking away from the dance floor and pulling me after him through the pub to the garden out the back, I'm pushed up against the fence and his lips crash against mine. All my oxygen is robbed, but I have his. This is our first kiss, and it's filled with promises my body wants to keep. The feeling of his lips on mine... I didn't know a man's lips could feel like that. Soft, full, smooth, heavenly.

Kissing and moaning, one hand is holding my head where he wants it, tilted and in place. This is not how it is supposed to go. I'm the one who is normally in charge, yet my body only wants what he can give me. His other hand stops at the bottom of my skirt, and he breaks our kiss. Opening my kiss-drunk eyes, I'm confused why he's stopped, what's happening?

"Lexi, can I touch you? Because it's taking all my energy not to finger fuck you right now?"

His eyes are surveying my face. I've no idea what he can see on my face. I feel drunk, but not from the alcohol. From his kiss. From his touches. From him.

Nuzzling against my neck, his words are slightly mumbled with his attention on the area where my collar meets my jaw.

"Yes." I move my head for more access. "God yes. Tonight, you can have all of me." I don't actually know how much of this man I want. But right now, I'll take anything from him.

His fingers are up under my skirt against my clit before our tongues have properly reintroduced themselves.

Rubbing me through my underwear right over my clit, the whimper that escapes into his mouth, hasn't happened in such a long time, that I can't believe it's coming from me. Every circle and rub over my sensitive nerves, are heightened to a point that only seems to happen with a vibrator, and he hasn't even touched my pulsating core.

I'm so wet, there's no hiding the moisture pooling in my underwear.

His lips haven't stopped connecting to mine. Our tongues continue to tangle and all while his fingers are playing me better than a fucking musical instrument. Gripping his shoulders, my knees are struggling to hold me up from sensation of pleasure his playing against my clit.

Pushing aside my panties, Marcus slides a finger through my juicy pussy lips and I nearly buckle when his textured finger drags the moisture over my sensitive nerves.

I've no idea how he knows how much pressure to add to my clit, but it's got me finding my own strength to grind down on his palm, while his fingers drive in and out of my centre.

"I'm coming. Fuck! Don't stop. Right there." His massage is thorough, and my orgasm comes hard and fast, coating his hand.

I pant from the high intense orgasm that he managed to rub out in minutes. He rests our foreheads together. Our eyes are closed, trying to regain a normal breathing pattern after that unexpected pleasure play.

"Lexi, I'm not doing anymore tonight." My confusion after that orgasm must be all over my face, when I open my eyes and look deep in his. "You're something special and I want to get to know you before I do more. And trust me I want more. Come find me when you're ready."

Removing his fingers from my quivering pussy, he lifts his fingers and sucks my essence from his digits. If that wasn't the best orgasm I've ever had up against a fence at the back of a pub, I would be wanting his tongue to gather the taste from the source.

With a promising kiss of more and my scent coating his tongue, which I take from him, he spins and leaves me quicker than my mind can comprehend. I'm panting, confused, horny and wanting more. I can't believe he is leaving me out here with a promise of wanting more.

Readjusting my skirt and discreetly putting my underwear back in order, I'm making my way back inside and I see him talking to Bea. His back is to me, but Bea's eyes find mine straight away.

I don't know what he's telling her. And I shouldn't care. However, what we just had was straight from my fantasy bank.

She turns into him to say something and I watch as he turns towards me and I freeze. Locked in a stare, I can see the mischievous twinkle in his eyes. With a wink to me and a kiss on Bea's cheek, he's heading for the door and what the fuck! Why would he be leaving when we just had that amazing time together. Then my orgasm fogged brain clears a little and I remember his words. *Come find me when you're ready.* How did he know I wasn't ready? But I was ready for a one-night stand. That's all I normally want... so why is my body telling me that maybe it's time for something more?

CHAPTER 4
MARCUS

Never in all my twenty-four years have I felt like this with a woman.

Sure, I've kissed, made out, brought them pleasure with my tongue or fingers, but never have I wanted anything more. Then in walks Lexi. Sexy Lexi. The noises that were escaping her as my tongue was dancing across hers and my fingers rubbing out her fast, explosive orgasm will forever live in my memory.

On the dance floor her body was all over mine and fitted better than any jigsaw puzzle. She's everything. I had to stop. I couldn't have a girl like that for a night. I'm not sure if it was pure lust, or the uncertainty of my experience with a woman. I just know Lexi is someone who interests the fuck out of me.

I saw how all those women admire and respect her when she announced herself in the group. That's power right there.

Leaving her panting up against the fence may not have been the best start to an 'us', but I need to know more. I've waited this long— a bit longer won't kill me. Although my hard cock in my jeans suggests otherwise.

The ever-perceptive eye of Bea catches me as I make my way toward her to say goodbye.

Grabbing her for a huge hug, my mouth is right near her ear. "I know you have questions, but right now I have no answers. She's more."

Bea sucks in a sudden breath "She's inside."

I break away and turn to see Lexi coming back into the pub. I wink at her, kiss Bea on the cheek and walk from the pub.

A best friend like Bea knows every emotion and understands that I can't talk about it now, but I also know she won't let me go more than a day without discussing this. Now we're in the same town, I dare say she'll be on my doorstep in the morning. The security is that Lexi doesn't know where I live yet, so she can't follow me and demand any answers. She only has my work address, after she kept my business card from our discussion earlier at the bar.

Once I make it home, I go straight to the kitchen, grabbing a beer from the fridge and looking around at the various boxes still to be unpacked in the living room of my house. I take a few heavy pulls on my beer and realise I may as well continue unpacking tonight. At least that will help to remove the fucking tent in my jeans.

Keeping my mind and body busy with productive exercises seems to be the best result for the uncomfortable feeling of Lexi swirling through my mind. Was I wrong to just leave her at the fence? How can I tell her I'm a virgin? She was so responsive and every moment I spent with her I wanted more and more. Bea hadn't really mentioned her, yet I felt like our connection was more than on a body level. It felt soul deep and that's what made it scary.

The buzz of alcohol has well and truly been burnt off with all the thoughts and to-do lists swimming around in my brain, and the focus of unpacking is keeping me determined to have this place looking livable.

Exhaustion finally hits a little before three and I collapse on my bed, face down and in a pair of sweats I changed into throughout the midnight arrangement of my new house. I'm pretty sure Lexi is the final thing that crosses my mind before there is nothing left but the darkness.

My body has the envious ability to ensure I can function the next day. Plus, my intelligence and previous escapades ensure I don't mix my drinks too much and I'm as good as new the day after a night out. Although I do need sleep. I'm not a complete robot.

So, whoever the arsehole is banging on my door at this ungodly hour had better have a good excuse.

Seven! Who the fuck bangs on someone's front door at this hour? I doubt it's Bea, she wouldn't do that to me unless she hadn't slept, pulled an all-nighter, and has to tell me about it.

Groaning I call out, "I'm coming. The dead are fucking coming with me. Stop bloody banging."

Pulling the door open I see Bea standing on the threshold with breakfast burgers and juice. "I should've known you'd only give me a day before gracing my new dwellings."

Sitting down at the dining table, we're savoring our breakfast meal when Bea asks, "is the business all set up? I didn't think that your house would be as organised as this."

The hidden mirth from Bea is something that I love about her. Straight to the point with all the hints of love and respect.

"The shop is ready to open on Monday. I did a bit of work yesterday after your messages and invitation. Flynn did an amazing job, it looks incredible. As for the house, I couldn't sleep."

"That would explain why you were grumbling at me banging on your door. Are you developing hangovers?"

The pretentious look in her eyes tells me she knew I'd be like this today. She knew I wouldn't have been able to sleep last night after meeting Lexi and she's just rubbing it in.

"No, smartarse. I'm not developing hangovers and you know it. But I'm telling you, she was the last thing I thought about before my head hit the pillow and the first thing I thought about when your banging woke me up. Speaking of which, why the fuck are you banging on my door at this hour? Or is this one of those stories I don't need to know about?"

Bea's smile is slow, moving from caring to pure vixen. "Well Sticks, I could tell you why I haven't slept." Wink. "I mean, I did pass out for a bit, but you can get squirmy from those stories. So, let's just leave it for now and focus on you."

Raising my juice in a salute of thanks for sparing me the details, we're back to our breakfast burgers.

I scrunch up all the wrappers and I turn to Bea to see, her eyes turn sympathetic to my feelings and her caring side is starting to come out. Thankfully, after more than a decade of friendship we can truly read each other.

"I saw you last night. Sticks, I get it and I know. This is no Bekky Kettleson. You and Lexi have something."

Of course she brought up Bekky, the girl in college that I thought I'd finally spend the rest of my life with. Until Bea found her hooking up with some random guy in the library stacks.

"Thanks Stones. But I left Lexi panting on the fence with the ball in her court. I told her if she wanted to do more she knows where to find me." Running my hand through my hair, I turn to my best friend. "Shit, what if I've already lost her?"

The frown on Bea's face is instant and I realise I've just said 'what if…' I expect the pinch that normally follows those two little words. It doesn't come and I know that whatever is coming, is worse.

For three years we haven't allowed ourselves to say 'what if…'. It's been do or die. "Marcus Cameron O'Brien, this one time I'm going to let that go, but I swear to all realms that you'll chase this and damn any consequences. We will not live a 'what if' life. I saw the two of you last night. I didn't want to push and I won't come between you or pick a side, but you guys have something. It won't hurt to follow that. If you get damaged from a broken heart, so be it. You've lived in the shadows and desires of a fairytale love story long enough. Just live, this one time."

Her stern warning has me building my courage and hope brick by brick. I know I will never let my best friend down. So, this week I'm going to Lexi and live my life.

CHAPTER 5
LEXI

I don't normally drink and definitely not as much as what I did Friday night when Marcus left. I composed myself, went back to the ladies and partied hard. I spent all day Saturday nursing a pounding headache and did not much else. I've heard Bea's stories of her drinking shenanigans and I'm fucked if I know how she does it.

Thankfully, on Sunday I was beginning to function again. I went into the gym for a light session and I swear my water bill is going to be twice as much with the amount I'd consumed trying to flush the toxins from my body. The weekend was a write-off after Friday night.

Mixed with every waking thought linked to Marcus and his sharp features, I truly can't wait for Bea to walk through the door today. I check the app to ensure she hasn't cancelled. Though, that woman is a workhorse and she loves every moment in here, even when she curses the ground I walk on some days. I've loved the last eighteen months since she came to the village and decided to stay.

Pulling up the boxing program for today's class, I look

and although it's been programmed for about three weeks, it's the perfect mixture of pain and sweat. Anything that hard will have Bea flipping her shit and that brings a welcomed smile to my face.

I watch the ladies come in chatting while wrapping their wrists and hands. Their eyes slowly drift to the workout and the groans are music to my ears. It's a partner boxing tabata workout with combinations before the core finisher that would have anyone's muscles screaming and burning.

Catching Bea's eye, I love the determination in her stare because I know she'll fight me right to the end, and she'll be doing it to better herself and boost the others around her.

"As you can see ladies, it's another partner session." Having done a quick head count and knowing from the app no more are due in the class, I set my eyes on Bea and she knows. I want answers and her muscles will burn because of it. "Bea, you'll be with me. The rest of you pair up and we'll start the dance between pleasure and pain."

Bea walks over to me with a booty band and a long resistance band. Her smile is just as knowingly evil as mine. For someone I've only known for a short time, our eyes share the information and understanding of an old friendship.

Squats and shoulder mobility movements give us enough time to start the conversation that needs to happen. "Bea, where does he live?" I ask in a voice low enough to know she can hear me, but no one else can. I don't want my private life published around the gym or town. I worry someone may have seen what happened with Marcus on Friday night, but that's not a problem for now.

Public information can lead to power in the wrong hands, and I've got to worry about Garry as well right now.

I know I could've messaged her for this information over the weekend, but I'm not hiding behind a screen. Besides I drove passed his workshop yesterday. I doubted he'd have an open sign in the window on a Sunday, but you never know if he's a workaholic or not.

"I'm not telling you."

"But..." The timer tells us to change to shadow boxing. Calling out to change, I still need to be a trainer, not just follow whatever desires Marcus stirred in my body. I don't even know what I really want from him. I just need to see him again. I redirect my focus to Bea. "You can't be serious? He told me if I wanted more, I'd know where to find him. How am I supposed to know that if I don't know where he lives?"

"You know where he works, go there."

She's saved by the buzzer that finishes the warmup. I love the sound of women awakening their muscles and feeling some pain from the personal gains they're achieving. Just showing up is an achievement I want them to acknowledge.

Snapping back into trainer mode I explain the workout. Upping the volume of the playlist, I put Bea through her paces. And what I knew only she could do: she puts me through mine. For thirty-five minutes Marcus didn't get a chance to enter my mind. If you're going up against Bea with gloves on, you have to be present. There is no slacking off when she's punching.

I look up as the timer counts down the final seconds and the buzzer sounds. Everyone drops and groans with satisfaction of finishing a grueling workout. But the five-minute core finisher switches with the timer and the groans are music to my ears, though my muscles are dreading the idea just like everyone else.

"Fuck off Lex, that's brutal."

I knew Bea wouldn't let me down. Partner taps and commandos are torture and truthfully, I didn't want the pain either, however, I wouldn't let my women down by backing out.

The cool down finally comes and I've never been more thankful to roll out my muscles in my life. In less than three days, my world has been flipped upside down and that workout put everything in its place. The burn in my muscles tell me I needed the sweat just as much as everyone else did.

People are starting to leave when Bea comes back to me. We gave each other space during the cool down, realising that we went extra hard on each other for the forty-minute workout. "Look Lex, you're one of my people and I cherish everything that we have, but he's my best friend. For most of our lives we've been each other's champion. So, trust me when I say, you'll see him. And soon. Don't give up on him because I won't give up on both of you."

Her wink and confidence that there is possibly an "us" leaves me with more questions than answers. Yet with no way to contact him except at his work, I'll trust this amazing woman and let time hand me my verdict about Marcus. And pursuing this seems too rushed and only infatuation. Anyway, I've got the problem with Garry to worry about, plus why would I want a relationship? That's not who I am. One and done. If he wants me, fine, but I don't chase.

The rest of the day goes off without incident, lots of sweat, paperwork and avoiding the thoughts of Marcus.

Going home after a long day, sleep is welcomed but quite sporadic. I try all the known ideas to help me sleep, they just don't want to cooperate. Guess it'll be another day of waking up tired.

After my morning classes and a quick trip home to refresh before returning to Fitness Freaks, I'm back on the gym floor because the office is too confining for my brain. I'm pushing my body through a grueling strength session before a PT class and then the Owl ladies' classes. They're the ones who enjoy evening classes.

The need to sweat Marcus out of my mind and body— even though I did the cardio sweat class this morning— is a strong one. Any break in my day brings thoughts of him to the surface. My brain just can't seem to switch off with how he made my body hum on Friday night.

My favourite music is so loud that it would give anyone a headache, but I need it to drown out any memories of last Friday. Since Bea's chat after class yesterday, occupying my mind with anything from a strength routine to catching up on the paperwork for the business is all I can do.

The best thing about a workout playlist is that the songs all blend, no breaks. It's also a problem when someone wants my attention.

An ear-splitting whistle cuts over the music and has me turning around to find Marcus standing there with a smug look on his face, eyeing my form.

Since starting this career, I've never been self-conscious of my body, but his gaze feels like it's stripping not only my clothes but going deep into my soul.

I reach down grabbing my drink bottle and towel before walking over to lower the volume.

"How long have you been here?" I ask.

Giving my body one last go over he replies, "Long enough to know you're both distracted yet focused on every movement."

"Well having you here is leaning more to the distraction side of things." I probably shouldn't put the sass in my voice, but this is my sanctuary.

His single raised eyebrow tells me that I've hit a nerve, but he's too much of a gentleman to call me out on it.

"I get that. I'm sorry. I thought you may have come to my workshop looking for me. Also, you mentioned Friday night you might do PT sessions, I'd like to sign up."

Taking a deep sigh and putting on my professional hat I say, "Follow me to my office"

I'd meant I'd started PT sessions with women, but I'd let him know in the privacy of my office, not on the gym floor. I have a PT session starting soon and not all the women are comfortable in the presence of a man.

He seems to be walking too close behind me as he follows me into my office. My body is reacting to his presence, hair raising on the back of my neck. Flutters through my stomach. Shivers of anticipation shoot up my spine.

My body is such a traitorous bitch. Why can't it take the hint? This man is quicksand. Shit, he left my panting body out the back of the pub last week.

Invading my space, I feel his breath on the back of my neck. "I've thought about you every spare moment I've had. No one has ever made me feel like this." He runs his hands up and down my arms while whispering. "Shit Lexi, I know I left things messed up, but you scared the shit out of me. I didn't know what else to do."

Feeling my body relax into his touch I muster all my strength, "What do you mean 'feel like this'?"

"We just have a connection, is what I'm saying."

I call bullshit, but right now my train of thought is all

over the place with everything that is going on. So why can't I kick him out?

I can't face him. Talking to the wall and letting my words make their way to his ears is much easier than facing him. His whole face will be broadcasting his emotions. That's something that captured me on Friday night, he wasn't hiding his emotions. "There are no male memberships available at my gym."

"That's ok, but I still want you."

Slowly turning, he allows me the space to move and look up into his eyes. Nearly sitting on the desk to get just a little more space between us. "Marcus, we've just met. Fuck, we don't even have each other's phone numbers, nor do we even know our surnames." Taking a deep breath.

"My surname is O'Brien." His face is registering my words and the confusion is evident. "Why not? Look I checked out the other gym when I came here looking for my business location and house. Your gym is a million times better and I haven't even used the equipment."

Smiling at his praise, it still doesn't change my ethos. "I appreciate your words. Thank you. Yet my ladies come here to feel safe and secure without the prying eyes of the opposite sex."

"So what does that mean for us?"

Wow, he's going there. Us? One finger fuck and mind-blowing kisses can't equal an us.

"Us? Marcus how can you say that. It's been less than a week. Look, I've got quite a bit on my plate right now and 'us', whatever you think that is, is not my priority."

Nodding, he leans in and my disloyal body automatically matches his energy and reaches out to him. "I'm not giving up." Kissing my cheek. "I'm not going anywhere." Kissing my other cheek. "And I'm going to make you see what having me in your corner means with the problems you're having. Because Lexi, I can't stay away." His lips seal over mine and I'm lost again in his kisses. Then he pulls away just as quickly as it all started and walks from my office.

That kiss has left me floating and it's only the sound of a weight dropping that I realise we're not alone.

Quickly regaining my professionalism and putting 'Sexy Lexi' back in her box, I'm out of my office watching Carly take her eye full of Marcus as he leaves. I feel a small pang of possession and jealousy, until I realise that Marcus didn't even acknowledge her. He would've known she was here, but he just left without even a glance in her direction.

I don't put Carly through her paces, just enough respect for value for money. She achieves a PB on her squats and her first set of chin ups unassisted. It's the little milestones that hold just as much weight as achieving the overall goal. You can't reach the main goal without the stones lining the path to achievement. And it's moments like these that I value and cherish my job.

The Owls for the six o'clock evening class start coming in as I'm packing up with Carly. All these women are here to improve their mind and body and I think joining them will help mine as well. Nothing like a bit more cardio and comradery to chase the nerves away.

The class is full of swearing, high-fives and encouragement as the scheduled workout brings everyone together and helps put me back in the right frame of mind.

Ushering the last of the women out, I see Bea waiting for me near her car, which conveniently is next to mine. "I told him to come and talk to you." This was not the declaration I was expecting.

Giving her the look of 'thanks, but fuck my life', she

throws her head back and actually laughs. Bea can certainly draw a smile and happily hold any attention. "That man has broken some hearts with his actions and yours did not need to be added to the pile. Especially when we got talking."

"Do I even want to know what you guys have been talking about?"

"I didn't tell him about Garry, if you're worried about that. But he did want to know if he could help."

"Thanks for the professional side. But you probably should've emphasised that this is a woman's only gym before he came."

"Maybe. But think about opening your membership."

Maybe she's right. But right now, a full day at the gym and Marcus showing up, I'm too exhausted to give a definitive answer. "Thanks Bea. But not now. This shit with Garry is playing on my mind. Have you heard of anything?"

She shakes her head, reaching for her keys.

"Sorry Lex. Nothing. But listen. He won't hurt you, and you'll be his first and I guarantee he'll be your last. That man loves with all his heart. Night."

Using every ounce of energy to school my features as Bea drives away after the bomb she just dropped.

He's a virgin!

Giving her a quick wave as she's passing me, I'm turning away so every muscle can be released. A twenty-four-year-old virgin. I'm fucking thirty-six. Twelve years difference and he's got no experience. What the fuck? Did she think we'd already discussed that much of our lives?

When you've spent your whole life in this town, it's a blessing for your body to be on autopilot to get you home. Pulling into my driveway, I have no recollection as to how I got here. All I can do is my best to tamp down my brain because it's going into overdrive.

CHAPTER 6
LEXI

If my gym is my sanctuary, my house is my haven. It was given to me when I came of age. I'd been living with Maggie while we finished high school. My parents had died in a car crash and because I was too young to live by myself, I moved in with Maggie and her family. Our parents were high school friends and practically family in every way except blood.

Our families were working class, never rich, but in love and life they were wealthy beyond monetary value.

Closing the front door to my family home, there is an ease that only comfort can give. Curling up in my favourite armchair, I feel like mindless scrolling before I refuel my body. I just want to stop for a bit.

Before I can even press on my app, there's a ping of an email coming through. It's nearly seven-thirty, why anyone would be sending me an email to my work account at this hour cannot be a good thing.

To: *lexi.monelli@freakfitness.com*

From: *garry.cawbourne@mayor.com*

Subject: Changed timeline

Opening it and with a quick scan, my heart sinks.

To Lexi,

From your vulgar display on Friday night, my original timeline has changed from six to four weeks.

Please start removing your equipment by the end of the week. My investor will be coming in on Monday to start measuring for his new fixtures and business.

Sincerely,

Mayor Garry Cawbourne.

This must be what drowning feels like. Fear can be like a living entity within your body and right now, I'm scared.

As I'm about to call Maggie, a text message from an unknown number comes through.

> **UNKNOWN**
> Tomorrow Bea will be fired, because she is your friend. You can't beat me, slut.

Screaming in fear, I throw my phone to the ground. I'm up and pacing my living room, trying to calm my racing heart and slow the cracks forming in my soul. I have no idea how to beat this horrible man.

With a little less rage coursing through my system, I

recover my phone and call Maggie. Once I've explained the situation, she is on her way over, stopping via the noodle shop. Normally my nutrition is on point, but right now, it's out the window like every other part of my life.

Twenty minutes later, two cars are pulling up my driveway. Cradling a cup of tea, I know Maggie has a key so I don't bother getting up to answer the door. Huddled under my snuggly blanket in my over-sized armchair, I don't even register who's with her until they're all standing in front of me— Maggie, Bea and Marcus.

He steps forward and places his hands on my knees and crouches in front of me. Rubbing small circles over my body, he says, "It's ok beautiful. We'll get him."

The floodgates open and sob after body-wracking sob tracks tears down over my cheeks. Marcus suffers the brunt of my tears being the closest to my breakdown. Maggie and Bea are adding comfort where they can; small circles on my back, rubbing my arms.

"Sorry, I..."

"Don't you fucking dare apologise." Bea says as we all get settled. "I was at Marcus' when Mags rung me, which is why we're here. And considering I'm supposed to be fired tomorrow, we may just need to pull an all nighter." I look at her with gratitude for being here when I realise, she didn't have to come.

She looks at Marcus, who has settled in front of me on the floor, rubbing my leg adding comfort. "Hey Sticks, what was the name of our school friend who became a detective?"

"Alfie Swanson?"

"Yeah, that's him. I'll track him down. Mags, what else do you need?"

Maggie looks just as shocked as me at Bea being all bossy. We'd always just thought her to be the fun, loving, party woman. It seems every person has their special and hidden talents.

"I'm good. I did have some files to go over and from the text message Lexi-Belle received before she called me, I'm actually going down to the police station."

"Wait." All eyes are again focused on me and this is going to break this issue right open. "I think I know why he's doing this."

Unfolding myself, Marcus moves back a little, while Maggie and Bea sit on the coffee table.

A few things had been swimming through my mind as to why Garry is doing this. Yet with that unknown text, likely to be from him, I better come clean about my thoughts.

Taking a deep breath, I find a spot on the wall beyond all of them to focus on. Going deep into my memories isn't always the best trip.

"I'd just turned twenty-one and could legally go to the pub. I'd sort of gained a bit of a reputation for a promiscuous lifestyle. Mags, you were at law school and well, I was here working at the gym and doing online courses. This one night, I'd been drinking a fair bit, when Garry and his mates came up to me. Being a couple of years older than us, he was good looking and had just finished his business degree. One thing led to another and I went home with him. A dick was a dick in those days and just another notch. We went back to his house but we never should have driven that night. We were so drunk." Lowering my head to whisper the punchline to the story. I swore to him, I'd never tell another soul and until tonight, I haven't told anyone. "He couldn't get it up."

A snort is what breaks the silence. Looking up I see

Maggie and Bea hiding a laugh behind their hands. Marcus is just smiling like the Cheshire Cat.

"What? He threatened to end my life if I ever told anyone. After all, his family is like royalty around here."

Struggling not to burst into fits of laughter, Maggie adds, "But you kept that from me, not only as your lawyer, but your best friend. Lexi-Belle, this is gold."

"Stop, yes, it's funny as fuck, but I took his threat serious. Look I was young and I never went back to try again. Even though he tried many times— even sober— to get in my pants, I always managed to avoid him and get away. Then as the years passed, he went after his power and found his now wife. I guess he still wants to hurt me."

"It's okay Lex," Bea is saying, "We're not going to share that secret, but we need to find out if his business partner is legit and if this has all stemmed from his drunken rejection. We'll let you rest and meet back here when we've got something." Standing up, Bea holds her hand out to Marcus, "You coming, Sticks?"

"Nope."

CHAPTER 7
MARCUS

All eyes turn to me. "What? I'm not leaving her." Both women are eyeing me in an unknown way. Perhaps trying to decide if me staying here is the best option.

Rising, I manoeuvre my way behind Lexi and cradle her in my lap before Maggie and Bea even leave the driveway. It feels like no one has snuggled up to this beautiful, strong woman in forever. It makes me want to hold onto her even more.

"Marcus, tell me something. Give me a story."

Kissing her head, it's comforting to wrap her up in my arms and kiss any part of her I can reach.

"My parents were childhood neighbours and the true definition of enemies to lovers, just without the violence books portray. They went to rival schools and their parents were competitors in business. They were always bickering. Until it changed. At a high school softball game, Ma was the star pitcher and Dad came up to bat. After two strikes, Ma deliberately walked him. He was pissed and all accounts, he stormed off to first base. After she walked the next batter, putting dad on second base, she unleashed her fury. Pitched and caught the batter, then threw to third and got Dad out for a double play which ended the innings. As they were leaving the field, he told her to meet him at his truck after the game. Let's just say that was the start of a beautiful relationship that saw me come into this world. They now live next to each other in a nursing home and although they're not yet fifty, dementia keeps them in need of care. They can't live in the same room because most days they're back in their childhoods hating each other over the fence."

She tries to bury deeper into my arms and I can't help but hold her tighter.

"Is that why you haven't given love a chance?"

Her question hits me a little hard, but she can't see my face. I was pissed at Bea when she came over earlier tonight and told me she'd all but shared my virginity secret with Lexi. It may not have been the blaring words – *Marcus is a virgin* – But saying she'd be my first is just the fancy equivalent.

"Yeah. Although the families were rivals, their love was mesmerizing to see. Even Bea's family show me that great love is possible. I had to move in with Bea to complete high school because my folks were showing early signs."

Turning in my arms so I can look at her beautiful face, she looks as though she has something to share with me. "I can't leave town." My face is neutral as I see in her eyes there's more to say. "My parents died in a car crash when I was fourteen and I moved in with Maggie's family until I was eighteen and this house – my family home – became mine. It's been more than twenty years and I've never made it pass the town limits."

Slowly moving in to give her time to pull away, I kiss her. Our foreheads are resting when she pulls away sitting in my lap taking deep breaths. I knew there was something special with this woman. Sharing a bond of having friends who are more like family than the ones we share blood with, is something not a lot of people understand.

"Okay, I'll give us a chance."

"Really?" My surprise is almost laughable if everything around us wasn't so morbid.

"Yes really. I've no idea what I'm doing when it comes to a relationship."

I cut her off. "Neither do I beautiful."

Chuckling, she says, "But with you, I want to try."

My first instinct is to lighten the mood and when is following your gut ever the wrong choice.

Lifting my hips, she bucks a bit and a sneaky grin is crossing my face. "*My* cock always works." I waggle my eyebrows for extra measure.

Shaking her head, she giggles before shutting that down. "Marcus, that is not even funny."

"Oh, I know. It's actually hilarious. But let me tell you. If I could've walked home last Friday night with my dick out, I would've. It hurt so much being trapped in my jeans. I think you better kiss it better."

A light kiss coasts across my lips like a feather, before she pulls back and rests her forehead to mine. "No baby, not tonight. It wouldn't be right. I appreciate you trying to change my train of thought. But just being in your arms is what I need." She snuggles deeper into my chest. "I haven't let anyone do this with me before, but I've given plenty of blow jobs."

There's no way I'd turn down being a first for her. "I've got you beautiful. My Sexy Lexi. Let's eat the noodles Maggie brought and we'll put a movie on while we wait for those two powerhouses to come back."

It's close to midnight when everyone is back at Lexi's place and lightly shaking us awake. At some stage, we'd left the armchair and made it to the lounge with Lexi mainly laying on top of me so we'd both fit.

Maggie looks positively glowing and Bea the opposite. This is going to be an information dump that we need to figure out how to deal with the Mayor and how to have Lexi happily and safely living in peace... with me. Because now that she's prepared to give us a try, I'm not ready to give her up.

Lexi says what I'm thinking. "Normally it's Bea that looks this happy, not you Mags. What happened?"

"Well, I took all the information into the police station just in case the wrong police officer was on duty, but it seems Lady Luck is coming to the party. Our friend, Buck Sawyer is on tonight and he listened to all the evidence I have against Garry, including the latest threat. We can't actually prove the text message, but he is issuing Garry with a restraining order in the morning. That should buy us some time to do more investigating."

With that news, we're all a little happier and it's easier to breathe.

Turning to Bea, I indicate for her to follow Mags.

"Alfie said he'd take the case, but it'll cost us." She takes a deep breath and I know my best friend. This is going to be hilarious. "Well me. I have to go on a date with him this weekend."

I can't contain myself. If Alfie resembles the geek he was in high school, I know he's not Bea's type. I crack up laughing. I mean we laughed enough when he became a detective.

Lexi smacks me in the belly and I groan a little. I knew

she had strength, I just didn't know how much. "Stop laughing at her. She's taking one for the team."

"No, he can laugh. I mean, I've never kissed anyone with glasses. He still looks like a geek. But it was worth it for us to get put to the top of his pile in the morning."

Maggie stands up and stretches, looking at her watch. "I think we've done all we can tonight, Lexi-Belle. I'll go unless you need me to stay."

Lexi shakes her head then gets up to give her best friend a hug and, truthfully, I'm left not knowing what to do.

Bea and I lock eyes and after spending so much time with her growing up, we're used to communicating without words.

Should I stay?

Whatever feels comfortable

Lexi is back from walking Maggie to the door and honestly, she looks dead on her feet.

"I'll stay if you want." I walk up to wrap my arms around her. The best thing is there's not a massive height difference. She fits perfectly under my chin. I can just wrap myself around her.

"Thank you. But I'll be okay. Besides I've got to be up in a few hours for classes."

"Ok. I'll give you my number. Call me no matter what. I'll be here for you."

Handing over my number, we hug and kiss again before I follow Bea out to her car. I never thought it'd be hard to leave someone's home. Watching her house disappear in the side mirror, I know there will be a time in the not-too-distant future where I won't be driving away from Lexi Monelli.

CHAPTER 8
MARCUS

Sleep certainly didn't come easily last night, but what I did get was heavy. Rocking up to work this morning, I'm only about eighty percent focused on my printing orders. Twenty percent is full of thoughts about Lexi.

Did she sleep ok?

How were her classes today?

What are her plans for the rest of the week?

How is she feeling about Garry?

I'm amazed the ratio of thoughts isn't higher to be honest. Being with her last night did reinforce for me the instant attraction I felt for her last week. In fact, it's grown from lust to affection.

Stopping around midday for lunch, I pick up my phone and notice a message from an unknown number. When I'm deep in the creative mode, I have to put my phone on silent.

Normally I delete them without opening, but as I click on the preview what I see has me freezing in my tracks.

UNKNOWN

Hi, it's L...

Quickly opening the message.

UNKNOWN

Hi, it's Lexi.

The time stamp is from about twenty minutes ago. This is so cute. I'm sure if anyone walked into the print shop right now, they'd see an ecstatic blush marking my cheeks. I didn't even know I could blush; this is new.

MARCUS

Hey, it's Marcus. You ok?

The smile on my face couldn't be removed by any force. I can't believe she messaged.

The three dots come up just as I go to put the phone down.

LEXI

Yes. I'm just messaging to thank you for last night and to ask if you want lunch. With me?

MARCUS

Food is an important part of daily living. That'll be nice. What do you have in mind?

LEXI

We could go to the café or my place. I'm actually finished classes for the day.

I know Garry should've been issued the restraining order this morning, so eating in public shouldn't be an issue. However, I want to build on whatever started last night.

MARCUS

> I like the sound of your place. Do you need me to get anything?

LEXI

> Meat and salad wraps are on the menu. If you want something else, grab it. Come by about 1.

MARCUS

> Sounds good

An hour. That's all I have to wait until I can see her again. My pulse has gone up a notch with anticipation of how to act when I get there. This is ridiculous. I've met royals and famous people, yet having lunch with Lexi, my palms are sweaty.

Finalising some orders and scheduling printing for the afternoon, I'm ready to head to Lexi's just before one. Jumping in Misty, I stop at the bakery to get an assortment of slices before heading to her house.

The purr of my 1966 mustang cannot be hidden. In its original glory, I carefully pull into Lexi's driveway and she's standing at the door with her hands on her lips.

She's frozen in awe.

"Lexi." I feel like I may scare her if I approach her too quickly. "Sexy Lexi, you okay?"

"That's your car?"

"Yeah, that's Misty. My grandfather bought it new. I'm the second owner."

"Fuck, she's amazing. I don't even think I could touch it."

Walking all the way up to her and kissing the side of her head because she's still frozen trying to take in all of Misty's features, I whisper to her, "Touch me instead."

I'm surprised she didn't get whiplash with how fast she turns to look in my direction.

There's mischief dancing across her captivating eyes. "I didn't know you could be that bold."

With probably a little bit of defensive sass, I say, "I may not have had my P in a V, but I know how to make you come." Throwing her arms around me and standing on her toes, she's kissing me with enough passion that I know this is not one sided. "Let's take this inside shall we." Smiling at my comment and shaking her head, she leads me inside.

Lunch is delicious and Lexi is a gracious host ensuring I've something to drink and the slices from the bakery are in the fridge.

There's been light touches and small kisses after the heated passion from my arrival died down enough over lunch. It just feels so natural.

The movies make it look so effortless to be sitting on the lounge making out. Our hands are cartographer's instruments mapping each other's bodies. Our shirts are off as I stretch my body over the top of hers and kiss every inch of her exposed skin.

Soft moans escape her heavy breathing when I suck her nipples through the soft cotton of her bra.

Between kisses and lightly sucking marks down her soft athletic middle, I gaze up at her. When I reach the top of her sports shorts, I ask, "Can I have a taste?"

"Don't you dare fucking stop." She lifts her hips to grant me access to remove her shorts and underwear. As I peel them down her legs, I'm hit with the scent of her essence and I can't wait any longer.

Diving back in, my face is buried deep between her thighs, licking her wet folds and flicking her clit.

She grabs my hair, holding me to where she wants the

most attention and I learn from her body. Licking around her entrance, I'm plunging my tongue in and out of her tight cunt, feeling little flutters of her inner muscles.

"Oh Marcus." She's throwing her head back and arching into my mouth. "Use your fingers. Fuck that feels good. I'm nearly there."

Doubling down from her instructions, I want to feel every clench of her muscles around my fingers, like I did last Friday night. It doesn't take long until she is screaming her release and soaking my face with her juices. I lap them up like I'm dying from thirst and she's my drink of water.

Glancing up, I still can't move with the strong hold she has on my head. She comes back down from her high and pulls me up her body. "I want a taste."

Fuck! That's the hottest thing I've ever heard and she doesn't have to tell me twice.

CHAPTER 9
LEXI

I've tasted myself off men before, a natural aphrodisiac, if that's your thing. And it is mine.

Running my hands up under his shirt I'm fascinated by the small ridges of muscles well earned. Lightly scraping my nails across his skin a moan escapes his lips.

"I never knew a woman's touch could be so addictive. I want you to do that again. All over my body."

Taking his instructions, I walk my fingers around his waist in a leisurely approach to his spine, slowly dragging my nails with each step. I've got all the time in the world and I plan on making the most of it.

With my lips back on his, the double stimulation to his body has moans invading my mouth with his tongue. I want all his sounds. That man ate me like his last meal. It's only fair I at least attempt to even the score. Two to zero is definitely one-sided and I need to show my gratitude.

Taking a breath, his hands are holding my face and I can see the lust building in his eyes when an alarm rings from the kitchen. Sounds of frustration and annoyance leave Marcus. "Fuck, I'm sorry, that's work. I have to go back and check on some printing I scheduled."

I can feel his erection twitching against my thigh as he's trying to remove his body from above mine. It's truly a battle of heart, body and mind. All warring in their own right, with none wanting to leave. And I feel the same way.

"Can I come?" His look is pure devious. "Don't look at me like that when it's your alarm going off. I mean, I'd like to see your shop."

Realising that this isn't the end of our time together, Marcus climbs off me and stretches his hand out to me. "I'd love that. We'll take Misty, but you'll need clothes."

Reaching down for my clothes that aren't too far away, I'm shaking my head. "Nope. She's too precious to just jump in and drive around. You have to appreciate the classic. I'll just wait here for you or drive myself."

He rolls his eyes at me. Can you believe he seriously just did that? It's both hilarious and an acknowledgement to just how old he is. I keep forgetting the twelve-year age gap, and the eye roll brought it straight to the forefront of my thoughts.

"Lexi, cars can be driven and appreciated at the same time. Just like women." Delivering that little speech with a wink, the concern of our age gap is stamped down.

"Oh, come on. You're supposed to be a virgin, yet you finger fuck, give head and know exactly what to say to a woman like a pro. I call bullshit. You're not a virgin." Now I'm fully dressed and we're heading to the door, I feel more confident in my speech.

All he does is laugh at me and holds the door open to his car. Muttering, I'm hoping he doesn't hear when I say "and a fucking gentleman."

He jumps over the door like they do in the movies and I

can't contain my shriek. "I swear Marcus, if you scratch this car because you want to impress me with stunts like that, I'll polish this car with your balls."

I'm greeted again with laughter. This seems like a comedy to him and a fucking suspense to me. I'm trying to loosen up, but all I seem to do is sit still, afraid any movement will tarnish or damage the beauty of this classic car.

Arriving at the shop, from the outside there are signs that life is being pumped into the old shell. A beautiful PRIperfectNT sign is mounted high above the door. Examples of his work filling parts of the windows which round out the promotional pieces and it all just feels like it's supposed to be here.

A bell chimes as we walk through and Marcus goes straight out the back behind the counter where there is a slight hum coming from the area through the saloon doors.

Taking in all the printing memorabilia and more examples of his work, I begin to appreciate his true talents.

Making my way through the saloon doors behind the register and counter, I see Marcus leaning over a computer with a massive poster print out next to him.

Wrapping my arms around him from behind, I kiss him between his shoulder blades and along his spine. "Your work is amazing. So talented." Every word is broken with a kiss.

"Thank you, gorgeous. I appreciate it."

Watching Marcus work, it's refreshing to see someone completely dedicated to their craft. It's like he can see the correct tones and shades of the colours and it's hot.

Marcus must be so captivated in his work that he doesn't seem to flinch from my touches, until I'm kneeling in front of him and undoing his pants. Reaching inside for his smooth cock. Whoever renovated this workspace certainly knew how to add hidden designs and aspects for 'naughty times' at the workplace.

"Fuck, Lexi. What are you doing?"

Kissing the tip of his cock, it's growing and getting heavier with all the attention I'm giving it.

"Trust me, you just keep doing what you're doing. I've got this covered."

"Lexi stop. What if someone catches us?"

Giving his now thick cock a light suck, I pop it from my mouth with a full grin. "If you want me to stop I will. Respect goes both ways. But no one will catch me here. Do you actually want me to stop?"

Sliding my hand up and down the smooth rod of steel, I stick my tongue out, resting his heavy cock on it. There's a small bead of pre-come sitting at the tip waiting for a taste. I lap at the taste of his masculinity and want more. His slightly salty taste has me looking up at him from my knees silently pleading with my desire to swallow everything he's willing to give.

"Don't you dare fucking stop." With a small thrust, I open wider to accommodate his size and have his cock at the back of my throat.

Stretching my lips, I relax my throat so I can take him deeper. Holding onto his hips, I control the depth and pace of his thrusts. Licking and sucking every glorious inch, I'm moaning with my own pleasure of giving this man head in his workplace where anyone could walk in and speak to him.

This is something I could get used to. That thought should have me running for the hills, but all it does is make me perform at my best.

Adding my hands to the action, it's not long before I can feel the tension building in his body.

I want it all. Every drop.

Rope after glorious white rope is being unloaded at the back of my throat and I swallow the lot, not losing any of it. Marcus is leaning heavily on the work bench, with deep breaths being sucked in, trying to regulate from that desired experience.

"Sexy-Lexi, I should've warned you I was coming, but I couldn't stop. Fuck that was amazing. My hand has never been that successful." Lifting me off my knees he has me up and sitting on the work bench. He stands between my open thighs. "Now let me taste."

Groaning with his return of my words to him. I waste no time letting him share the flavour.

When all our air has been swapped along with his taste, snuggling with him between my legs is a natural feeling I didn't think would ever come with such ease.

"What now my Sexy-Lexi?"

Looking at the huge clock on the wall, it's nearly time to close the gym. "I've got to go and lock up Fitness Freaks soon. We could leave here, go there for a workout because no women will be there— I pride myself of privacy. Then what do you say about dinner at my place?"

"Everything about that sounds perfect. Give me thirty minutes to finalise everything and I'll be free, then we can just drive to the gym. You can chill out on the lounge in the waiting area or wherever you want to wait."

Giving him a light kiss, because anything more and one of us will be giving the other another orgasm, I get off the bench and go out to the waiting room stretching out with a magazine to wait.

The drive wasn't long from the print shop to the gym,

and aside from Misty being a classic, I'm still not that used to being in a car with someone other than Maggie.

Allowing Marcus to walk ahead of me, I lock the doors so no one can come in while we're in here. There are no classes or 24-hour access anyway, but you never know.

Loading up a workout playlist, I start to set out sandbags, kettlebells and dumbbells. He's just standing there watching me set the equipment out in a circuit situation with a mysterious look on his face, like he's never seen stuff like this before.

"I don't see a workout plan. Lexi, should I be worried?"

I sway my hips a little more as I walk up to him. "Oh baby, I'm going to make you sweat. You're in my house now."

I can see the lust coat his eyes and he makes to grab me but I step away. I'll have to keep my head about me, otherwise he may just be punching that V card on my gym floor.

Putting my professional hat on I explain the circuit. "I'll set the timer for thirty minutes. Starting at twenty reps for everything, we'll see if you can make it to zero within the time frame. Sandbag, backloaded squats. Cals. Kettlebell alternating swings. Cals. Dumbbell thrusters. Cals. Then drop by five after each set. Take your rest when you need it."

His eyes are bugging out as I go through each example with a little demonstration.

We warm-up, stretching a few muscles and adding in mobility movements that will be getting a good workout throughout the session.

"You ready?"

"Gorgeous, I won't give up. But Lexi, if I can't walk after this you have to drive Misty home."

Shaking my head, I know my face is shocked at his announcement. "Second thoughts, just watch me. I'm not driving that car." Fuck, I can't leave town, let alone drive a classic like Misty. Chuckling we're lining up behind the sandbags as the countdown timer starts.

For the next thirty minutes we do the workout with encouraging words and praise as each round passes.

When the final three beeps countdown to the last buzzer, we both drop our weights and groan in exhaustion. With a high-five, we're panting on the floor. I probably could've gone with something easier, but this is the easiest to set up and explain.

"How are you feeling baby? You surprised me by keeping up with me and all that. We need to cool down though. A few stretches."

"My God woman, do you have a whip as well? Ease up and just let me die here."

Rolling towards him, I say, "If I have a whip, I'm not using it in public." Standing up, I reach down to help him up. "I know, but stretching will help."

With the roller, ball and basic body stretches, I can see the ease of his body. This is my favourite part of a workout. The satisfaction of completing a workout and stretching all the muscles out. Too many people skip this part and I swear they pay for it later.

Marcus helps me set up for tomorrow morning's classes and we're leaving as the sky is changing colours. Looking out the sun is heading towards the beach. In the peak of summer the tourists and locals flock to the shore trying for the best pictures. This season feels different already. Walking toward Misty and Marcus, the tides are turning. Maybe he is the future I didn't know I wanted. But the age gap, his adventurous lifestyle and lack of experience is having me questioning why this is the right move.

Then he puts his hand on my thigh as we're driving to my house for dinner and a warming glow passes through my system. Maybe this is right. Father Time is the one holding the answers.

We pull up to my house and for the first time ever I can see myself sitting on the porch waiting for him to come home.

It can't be love, but there's certainly chemistry. From our stories about our parents, genetics suggest we're due for a future that's worthy of a storybook ending. Yet making the start and taking that first step is causing havoc on my nerves.

CHAPTER 10
MARCUS

I didn't know life could feel like this. I've experienced joy and happiness before with work, travel, and personal achievements. Yet just being with Lexi... I've never felt peace like this. When she went down on me in my shop it was a thrill completely different to the rush of a roller coaster. It was naughty, pleasurable, exhilarating knowing we could've been caught at any moment.

Then a gym session of grueling punishment which was physically rewarding. I'm still buzzing from that high.

The crazy thing is, this has all only been in an afternoon. Spending the time with Lexi feels natural, like it's meant to be.

We briefly stopped at my place to get a change of clothes, before ending up at Lexi's family home. It shouldn't be comforting to know she understands what it's like to not have parents around. Granted mine are in a care facility a few hours away, however every time I go to visit them, I have to do it separately. Ma thinks I'm someone from her softball team and Dad thinks I'm a mate from his math class. Our discussions are pleasant enough, but most of the time I just want them to remember their love.

Hanging my head against the pressure of the shower, I should really get out and help Lexi with dinner. The sudden drop in water temperature is what helps me make the decision.

Running since high school, then as a coping mechanism with my parents' early diagnosis, I'd consider myself a fit person. But that workout Lexi pulled from her arse this afternoon found new muscles and tightened old ones.

Coming out to the kitchen, the aroma of a home cooked meal is nearly too much to handle. The scent of spices is hinting at the masterpiece she's building.

Coming up behind her, I wrap my arms around her waist and peer into the concoction on the stove. "What's cookin' good lookin'?"

It feels like the most natural thing to do. And she eases into my grip like we've been doing this for months. Not less than a week.

"Fully loaded stir-fry. Quick, easy, nutritional. I should've asked if you have any allergies. Sorry." I kiss the top of her shoulders and even through her T-shirt it still sends comfort and warmth to every inch of my body that I can do this simple action to her.

She just fits.

I know her inability to leave the town could be an issue, but that's a future problem. Right now, it's getting through this meal without laying her on the table and discovering the missing piece of my soul.

"No allergies gorgeous. Sounds delicious. Is there anything I can do to help?"

"You can set the table." She directs me to where everything is kept. This is pure domestic bliss. Making meals. Creating memories. Light touches and kisses whenever we're near each other.

Sitting facing each other, the conversations are easy, ranging from high school stories, my travels, her anecdotes from working in the fitness industry for nearly twenty years.

Moving from the dining room to the lounge room, I get flashes of the last time we were in this room. It's hard to believe it was only last night. It feels like ages ago with the lightness and ease of what being together creates.

We're watching a movie and Lexi is snuggled into my side with her fingers lightly dancing over my abdomen. Whether it's on purpose or not, every so often she grazes across my cock making it twitch a little bit.

"Sexy-Lexi, I can't take it anymore. Stroke my cock or suck it, just stop teasing it."

I know she can hear me; I didn't mumble or whisper, but she doesn't stop her actions or cease the grazing across my now tented tracksuit pants.

I've lowered the barriers to my mind and heart and all I can think about is making Lexi mine. Broken heart or not, I want this woman.

Her grazing has increased to stroking through the material with her eyes turning to mine from the screen. Our breathing has increased and matches each other.

I lower my hand down over her shoulder to start my own exploration of her body. Feeling muscles and trying to give her breasts the same quality time she's now showing my dick.

Her nipples are such hard pointed peaks that I'm surprised they aren't breaking through the material. Tweaking, twisting and lightly pulling her nipples brings a wanton moan from her lips.

"I want another taste. Marcus, will you let me?"

Her hand slips below the waistband, and her guttural groan of discovering that I'm commando has me using my hips in a silent permission for her to do whatever she wants to me.

With her mouth wrapping around my throbbing cock, I'm back to thinking of anything to stop the enviable.

"Fuck, that's so good," I moan, resting my head on the back of the lounge.

She removes her mouth with an audible pop and is hoping off the lounge to lower her own sleep shorts.

"I want you. If you want to take this to the bedroom to have your first time there, say so. Or God, let me ride you and give you the best feeling of your life." She's still stroking my hard, smooth cock with beads of pre-come sitting at the slit. "Do you want to use a condom? I'm clean, I get tested regularly and I can't get pregnant."

"Bend down and lick my cock." She answers my command with the action. Lust and desire are radiating from her eyes. "I want to feel you fucking bare. I don't want anything between us. Now fucking climb on and fuck me like you want. Make yourself come so hard you can't walk from my big cock stretching you out."

Removing all her clothes, I take mine off and staring at her strong curvy figure has more pre-come leaking from my bulbous tip.

She straddles my thighs as I hold my cock at the base and watch her slowly sink down over every hard inch.

She's so wet and her inner muscles are twitching as she finally sits all the way on top of me.

Our foreheads resting on each other and sharing the same air, I need to speak.

"Gorgeous, I'm not going to last. But I'll do my best to make it good for you." I move my dick the smallest amount.

Any movement from her has me sucking in deep breaths to make it last for her.

"You are so fucking big. Fuck you fill me." Rolling her clit over the base of my cock has both of us groaning in pleasure. "I'll make this good for both of us. Just follow my lead." She rolls her hips again, and I'm so fucking close. "Now grab my arse, follow my rhythm, and suck my tits. If you want to leave a mark on them. I'm yours."

We're so still it's like we've been blasted with a frozen ray gun.

I'm yours.

She knows what she's just said, and my reaction is what will make or break this moment.

"Fuck me Lexi. Fucking claim me."

That's the only instruction she needs. Filling my mouth with one of her tits, I suck deep and hard knowing I'm leaving a mark on her flesh, and it makes both of us rock and thrust a little bit harder.

Squeezing her arse, I know I'll leave fingerprint shaped bruises there as well. Not that anyone will ever see this woman naked again. She is mine, all mine.

Popping free of her beautiful tits, I roar my release just as she throws her head back and screams her own pleasure all the way to the heavens. She collapses on top of my chest. I'm holding her tightly, not wanting anything to come between us. I know there will be a mess when I finally pull out, but I can't bring myself to care. This amazing woman has just punched right through my V card all the way to my heart.

Our breathing has returned to slightly normal when she finally climbs off me. Our combined mess leaves her swollen pussy, sliding down and gathering around my thick cock.

Fuck, I shouldn't want to fuck her straight away, but that is so fucking hot to see.

"We better clean up." Kissing me, she steps back enough to allow me to stand up before putting her hand in mine and leading me to her bedroom and the ensuite just off the side.

Lifting Lexi up to the basin, I place her there while I get a washcloth from the shelf display. Running the warm water over the cloth, then placing it over her sensitive pussy. Being gentle, I say, "That was amazing." There are a few different colours across her breasts. I shouldn't see it as a badge of honour, but I loved staking my claim to her flesh.

"Marcus," she's cupping my face looking deep in my eyes. "I got carried away and I used your huge cock to my advantage. I'm ok. How are you feeling?" Looking down at her chest, there's a smug look on her face. "I'd say you're feeling rather proud based off these marks?"

It's like my mouth has no filter as I just say the first thing to come out. "You've wrecked me for any other woman. Just as well there won't be any others, because I just want you."

Her whole body is sated from the passion on the lounge, but I see the flicker of uncertainty cross her eyes. There one moment, gone the next. Kissing her, I'll take anything I can tonight.

Pulling her off the counter, her legs naturally wrap around my waist and I carry her back to the bedroom. I didn't think I would be able to recover and consider another round, but my cock has other ideas. With her pussy lightly grazing my six pack as I walk back to her bed. She is starting to moan again while she has her head buried in my neck.

Lowering her to the bed, I lay over the top of her. Kissing along her collarbone and licking across her neck.

She's withering under me looking for friction to ease her pussy that feels wet against my abs. "You've had a full-on couple of days. Are you sure you want to go again?"

She moves her lower body just enough to let me know that I may have overestimated her recovery time. "If you do all the driving this time and take control, I think we might be able to fit in round two, maybe even more."

"How about I start by kissing you better and we go from there." Kissing down her body, I'm at her pussy, all pink swollen lips and I kiss and lick her until she's feeling so wet there wouldn't be a lot of resistance for me to push back inside.

Slowly rising I aim my cock at her entrance, it is more perfect than the previous time. Will it always be like this? Fuck, no wonder people rave about how glorious sex is and especially a woman's pussy. I'm an addict. All I want is this beautiful woman. All of her. Daily.

It's moments like these I realise why I sleep with my phone on vibrate. Although, when I was in Europe and the time difference to Bea, I wouldn't put it on vibrate. The ringing is not irritating factor here, it's the fact I'm wrapped in a warmth which I've never felt before and I have to move to reach my phone.

At some point after the second or third round, Lexi and I had gone back to the kitchen, had apple pie, in which I ate the cream from her pussy and not the spoon, but we'd retrieved our phones as well.

Untangling my limb from hers, I reach the bedside table and see it's an unknown number. Well, whoever that is can go fuck themselves. Placing it back on the table, it stops ringing, only for it to start again immediately.

"For the love of sleep answer the fucking phone Marcus, or I will throw it into the middle of next week." I shouldn't be smiling at the threat from Lexi, who is trying really hard to burrow deeper into my side.

"Whoever the fuck this is, you better have a good excuse to be calling at this hour." There is no need to be friendly when woken by an unknown person.

"Thank fuck you answered. I wouldn't have stopped anyway. It's Alfie, Alfie Swanson. Bea has been in an accident. She was on her way to see me. I had information for her and she had a car accident."

In an instant, I'm up and looking into the darkness trying to make sense of all he's telling me. "Where Alfie? Where is she?"

"They've taken her to the major hospital. I'm here now. She's in a medically induced coma. And the only reason they are telling me this is because I'm throwing around my badge."

"I'm on my way. Thanks. Please stay with her until I get there."

A soft hand on my shoulder brings me back to the present and I realise I'm still in bed with Lexi. Turning to face her, I know she's heard everything. There's a war crossing her face for the uncertainty of what she can do or what I will do.

"I have to go to her. Will you come with me?"

"You know I can't leave the town. I've tried. Maggie has tried. I just can't." She hangs her head in defeat and I have no idea the pain she is going through right now. This strong, powerhouse of a woman is letting distance and trauma rule her life. In time, I will fight those demons with her. But until then, I can't be here. I know there is fuck all I can do with Bea in a coma, but I need to be with her. She has been with me through all the shit with my parents and never once did she not fight for me. Now when she's unable to fight for herself, I'll do it for her.

"Gorgeous, I have to go. Bea has been there for me through everything. I'll call you. Promise, no matter what, you'll pick up. I'll keep you posted as much as I can." Kissing her, I've never felt so torn in my life. One night in her bed and I know this is the bed that I want to sleep in every night and she is the woman I want to wake up next to every morning.

I get dressed and walk back to her side of the bed. "Go back to sleep gorgeous, I'll call you between the Sparrow classes and the ladies at nine-thirty."

I love you

It shouldn't be said this soon, but everything is pointing to those three words. With more restraint than I knew I had, I pull away from Lexi, who is sitting in bed with the sheet pulled up to her chin and tears falling down her cheeks.

CHAPTER 11
LEXI

Never have I felt so weak and drained or had such hatred for my inability to leave town. I didn't think about why I couldn't leave, I just didn't do it. As time passed, things would happen and it wasn't until months, sometimes years later, another incident would pop up and I'd either come up with a creative way to get around the fact that I couldn't leave town or I'd pick myself up and build a fucking bridge to get over it.

However, listening to Misty purr down the end of my street right now, I hate every atom in my body which has me frozen in my bed in anger and fear. The war going on in my body over the fear of leaving and the possibility of losing Marcus and Bea is so strong that I throw myself into the pillows and scream until I'm hoarse.

Looking at my phone, it's an hour until I'm needed in the gym for the first of my Sparrow classes and I know nothing will happen here in that time. Getting up, I'm dressed, with a spare set of clothes and out at my car ready to do the only thing I know in this situation: keep fucking moving.

Pulling up at the gym, I have everything set up for the class, so I just go into the boxing section, wrap my hands and let my fists fly. The frustrations of not being able to leave. *Jab, cross, jab.* The fact that Garry may not be able to physically come near me, but can still hurt me. *Jab, cross, upper cut.* The fact that Bea was going to see Alfie for me. *Jab, cross, hook, upper.* Every punch there is a new face, a new pain that I want to eradicate. I've set a timer, otherwise I would've kept going long past the burn set to inflame my muscles.

With enough time to change into a fresh set of clothes, I'm back out on the floor before the first of the members are walking through the door. And like I've done many times before; I refocus my life. No longer is this about me. For the next two hours, my thoughts and actions are ensuring every woman who walks through that door leaves in a better headspace than what they came in here feeling. Right now, the women in my classes are my priorities.

Marcus leaves me a text message while I'm in class.

MARCUS

> Hey gorgeous, I'm here. I'll call you after Sparrows xxxxo

A minuscule feeling of pressure has been lifted knowing that he's safe and he'll call me once I can talk. The classes are successful, and no one mentions that Bea is not here. Although we get used to certain members in the class, we never pry as to why they may not be here. Not everyone can make a five am class.

No sooner has the final member left from the last Sparrow class, than my phone rings. Seeing Marcus' name, I answer.

"How is she? How are you?"

"It's so good to hear your voice, even though I heard all varied volumes of it last night."

"Are you seriously flirting with me when your best friend is in a coma?"

"Yep. What else am I supposed to do? She is doing ok. The doctors are saying she is likely to be in the coma for three days, depending on the swelling. I was talking to Alfie when I arrived and he said he'd send the information he found through to Maggie."

"I feel terrible. It's my fault. I can't leave here. I can't be there with you or Bea." I'm glad he can't see how dejected I feel. This is why I can't form relationships; I'm not even a whole person.

"Listen to me. This is not your fault." The authority in his voice doesn't match his young age. At least it helps to remove some of the helpless feelings. "I understand. There is nothing you could do here except sit with me and Bea. And I'm not up to PDA in the unlikely event that she wakes up. But even medical staff don't need to see the things I'd do to you."

"Seriously, you have to stop." I smile, because he really is relieving the load of the uneasy feeling that has been coursing through my system since he left in the small hours of this morning. "What have I turned you into? One night of sex and you're talking PDA and mentioning the volume of my sex voice." It feels good to joke. Though, is it just a mask?

"Whoever I am it doesn't matter as long as you love who I am."

Fuck, he just mentioned the L word. The worst part is, I feel it as well. I feel his love, his devotion, his want to be mine forever. Is this what I want? Last night it was brewing. Nevertheless, I'm here, he's there and there's a twelve year age gap.

"So, what do you plan on doing today then?" Yeah, I chicken out. I'm not talking love at this hour or in this situation. It's bad enough that in the heat of passion last night I told him to claim me.

"I plan on doing some work with my laptop while hopefully my arse doesn't go numb in the plastic seats. They really don't like people who aren't sick in hospital. Do you have a full day in the gym?"

I'm thankful we've stepped away from the love and sex talk. "Yeah, I'll be here all day. Though I might ring Maggie for lunch and just see where we're all standing with the whole Garry thing."

"Okay gorgeous, I'll let you go. Please call me if you need anything and I'll let you know if anything changes with Bea. You're mine."

Is that his way of saying, I love you? In this moment, it feels more powerful. Everyone says 'I love you', but is there any weight in those words? *You're mine,* seems to make things final. "See you, baby."

I couldn't say it. When the line goes dead in my hand, I'm searching myself to try and understand why I didn't say it back to him. I couldn't. There's too much uncertainty in my life right now.

Deep in thought and reflection, I don't hear anyone in my gym until a weight is dropped and the sound registers in my office.

Shaking myself and going out, I look at the clock and realise no one should be in here, however it is not unheard of for a member to be in here during opening hours.

The real shock is that there's a man standing over near the frosted window with a tape measure in hand.

"Excuse me, what are you doing here?"

The man turns around and all I see is surprise that he's been caught. "The door was open, I just let myself in."

"I can see you did that. However, you must have missed the sign that says *ladies only*. This is a women's only gym and men are not permitted without speaking with me first. So, I'll ask again, what the fuck are you doing here?"

Normally I wouldn't swear, but I've had fuck all sleep, great pleasure, personal pain and have no patience for strangers in my gym.

"Right, well I'm Emmanuel Beigh, Garry Cawbourne sent me to measure out the space."

"Are you the silent partner?"

"Miss, Garry contacted me three days ago to come here and measure this space for the laundromat he wants to put in."

His neglect at answering my silent partner question has me redirecting my questioning. "Garry told me I would have until Monday to start removing my equipment. You seem to be here a little early."

"He didn't tell me anything about a timeline. Just told me to be here today."

This is beyond frustrating. I need a fucking break. "Listen Emmanuel, I understand that you have a job to do to measure up for your laundromat, but you can't be here at the moment. You can come back after hours, but I really don't feel comfortable having you in here when one of my members could come in."

"Sorry, Miss, but it's not my laundromat. I'm just the one doing the measuring."

Getting a good look at him, he doesn't fit the

tradesmen's mould. He's in clean slacks with a polo shirt and no insignia saying which company he's from. "So, who are you working for again?"

"I told you, I'm here because Garry Cawbourne needs this place measured up. I'm actually just an actor he's hired. I know nothing about laundromats or anything. I've just got to report back to him with a few measurements."

This is not adding up. I wish I had someone here with me, but Marcus is with Bea, and Maggie wouldn't be up yet. I guess this is all going to have to be down to me.

"Emmanuel, I'm not too sure you're aware of what is happening here. Can you please come into my office so we can have a chat? If for no other reason, I don't want any women to see you. This is their sanctuary and I won't have that peace destroyed."

Stepping aside, I gesture for Emmanuel to enter my office.

"You know, this is a great facility, I'd love to come to this gym."

"Glad you like it, but right now it's just for ladies." Gesturing to the spare chair in my office, I say, "Have a seat." Sitting across from him, I motion for him to start talking.

"As I said, Garry approached me three days ago asking if I would do a small acting job for him. He needed me to pretend to be a businessman and come in and measure the space for a laundromat. He said he'd have the space by the end of the month."

Holding up my hand to stop him, I have a few questions. "Firstly, why would you do the job for him? Secondly, why are you telling me this?"

"I did the job for him, because to measure this space, look like a businessman and report back to Garry with any other information I have from within these walls he is going to pay me two thousand dollars. Now, the reason I am telling you this, is it may just be the last thing he does. When I was speaking with him yesterday to get the information needed for this gig, I overheard him saying, 'I'll take her out no matter what.' Whatever it was, I didn't like it. So, I questioned him a little and found out he was preparing to create an accident of some sort."

"Wait, you can't be serious?"

Shrugging his shoulders like it was just another Thursday, "That's what he told me. You must have done something pretty serious to have this man attack you like he is?"

"That's not important, nor is it my fault." My mind is flying around in all directions trying to figure out what to do next. Where do we go from here? "Emmanuel, thank you so much for coming clean and realising that Garry is not a nice person. What will you do now?"

A crooked smile crawls across his mouth. "I'm going to go to my motel room and draft a report, so it looks legitimate. Then go to his office, tell him that the space is perfect for a laundromat and dry cleaners. However, we both know my report won't even be worth the paper it is written on. But I want my money."

"That doesn't really help me now, does it? So, Emmanuel, how is that going to stop Garry from kicking me out of my gym?"

His crooked grin has now formed into a full evil smile. "Because Miss Lexi, I know it is all fake and I know just who to talk to while my pockets stay full," He says, tapping the side of his nose for good measure.

Nodding and standing, he reaches out his hand towards me, shaking it he says, "I hope you get through this unscathed. That man does seem do have a lot of power. Good luck, and if you need anything just let me know or call me when you turn this into an open gender gym." Handing over a business card, he walks out as the ten o'clock ladies start to walk in.

They're all murmuring and it doesn't take a genius to realise they're talking about Emmanuel. "Look, stuff is happening, but don't worry. You are my priority for the next sixty minutes, so get ready to sweat."

I've never wanted to close my gym early or kick them out as much as I do in that class. It takes all my energy to stay focused and not end up herding them out so I can go and see Maggie.

It's closer to the middle of the day when I finally get to Maggie's office. I thought I better go back to my house and quickly get something to eat and half decent clothes, not just workout attire.

Knocking on her door and waiting for the invitation to come in, it doesn't take me long to see that she has a lot on her plate and I hate that any amount of it could be my case. There are tired circles under her eyes, stress lines around her mouth and at least three coffee cups on her desk.

"Mags, this doesn't look good. I'm sorry."

She holds up a finger, her sign to shut it real quick. "Nope, you won't apologise for me becoming a darn fine lawyer or for the fact that Garry Cawbourne is just below a motherfucker."

Wow, Maggie swearing before the sun's down is not like her. If she's been drinking, she can put a soldier and sailor to shame, but professional Maggie in her office is not the potty-mouth who just let's it out. Sitting down, I watch as she takes a few calming breaths.

"Are you ready to tell me what has happened?"

"You look really nice by the way."

"Mags, have you slept?"

"Not properly in a few days. Actually, I'm not sure what day it is. Every time I go to put my head on the pillow, something comes into my head and I have to investigate. You know what I'm like. This is why I don't think I could work in the big city on the big cases, I wouldn't get sleep without pills and you know how much I hate taking those."

Reshuffling her pages, she goes to take another sip of coffee, before realising that's not the best option.

It's best I tell her why I'm here, even though she probably knows. "Bea is in the hospital. She was hit last night in a car accident. Marcus was with me when he got the call from Alfie Swanson." I'm looking at my hands the whole time I give the speech. It's nothing embarrassing, and Marcus may have told me that it's not my fault Bea is in the coma, but that hasn't helped much of the guilt subside when I'm looking at my best friend and family being shredded from the workload linked to my case.

"Well, I did not know that was where Marcus was last night. I did know about Bea though. Alfie rang me this morning at a stupid time. I was up anyway." Raising my head I look at her in time to see her eyebrows wiggle. "You going to tell me what it was like fucking a virgin?"

Collapsing my head in my hands, I'm mumbling and groaning before raising up to look her directly in the eyes, "It was the best sex I've had in...anyone's guess." The smile on her face is absolute wicked. "But I still couldn't get over the fear and go with him to the hospital. Although when he rang me this morning he signed off with 'you're mine'."

Throwing her hands up and swinging back on her chair, she is cheering to the ceiling. All I can do is smile and let out a little giggle with how quickly she can change and turn anything into a positive.

"Well before we get into the juicy details, let me tell you what I've gathered about our lovely Mayor."

Maggie proceeds to tell me that Garry had quite a few debts under his belt and that he needed his parents to bail him out before he became Mayor. Once that happened, the slate was cleared and he could start fucking up again. Only this time, he was using the taxpayers and government money and his parents couldn't do shit. Fraud is a hard thing to hide, unless you know how to and according to her sources, he is shit at hiding things.

"I've bundled up all the information into a lovely little package and I've sent it to Alfie who has better connections than little old me, so he's going to hand it over to the people who know how to deal with people like Garry, instead of the fuckwhit in charge of our police. Although, he probably won't be there too much longer either. Him and Garry make strange bedfellows. At least good old Buck isn't involved."

Every time she mentions the terrible things Garry had done that led to me being his next victim, or perhaps an easy target, I feel the weight lift a little from my shoulders. By the end of it, I feel like I have the courage to ask for the one thing I know only Maggie can do for me.

"I need to get to Marcus. I need to tell him that he's mine too." It's a rush as every word is pushed out of my mouth and slamming together. "Mags, I'm sorry, but I need your help. Can you please take me to him?"

It's only now that I realise how true those words are. He really is the one who has the power to drag me from this town. Knowing that Garry is getting closer to his demise, my gym will be saved and Marcus will be here for as long as his business is here. Plus he makes me happy. It wasn't just the sex, although orgasms are a great start to a relationship.

She's standing before I can even finish the sentence. "Of course, and to take your mind off the long-arse trip, I want every detail about your time with the young designer."

A blush creeps over my face and heads down over my whole body. It feels like it's on fire with the unknown of leaving town and not knowing what I will find when I get to the hospital.

CHAPTER 12
MARCUS

Hospitals are never a fun place for anyone. Even the people sitting next to their loved ones don't want to be here anymore than the people in the beds.

Yet here I am sitting here for the fourth day listening to the sounds keeping Bea alive. Beeps linked to her heart. Compressions for her lungs. It's quite real that in a flick of switch something could drastically change. The doctors came in yesterday to determine if the machines should be turned off. However, the swelling hasn't reduced enough and it's a day-by-day situation now.

The medical team have been great allowing me to sit here tapping away on the computer. When they discovered that her family were away on holidays and that I had all but been adopted by the family, they allowed me to stay.

I haven't heard from Lexi since the first day. I've sent messages, but they remain unread. I've called, but that just goes straight to message bank. I'm torn.

Bea is my past, my best friend. Lexi, I thought, was my

future. Sitting here, neither are my present. It's just my thoughts and the machines keeping me company.

Alfie has been popping in checking on Bea, and inadvertently me. We've swapped a few stories about high school and what people have been up to. However, Bea was my only consistent in the years since, so I can't really add much to his conversations.

I can see his affection for my larger-than-life best friend beeping away near us. I know he's not her regular man, but no one else has been to see her or called. The glasses, and the start of salt and pepper colouring through his hair, gives off silver fox vibes. At twenty-five it may not attract a lot of women, but he's done nothing but protect and be in our corner since Bea reached out to him when all of this started.

He has to leave for work, but says he'll call later today and asks me to message if Bea's condition changes.

I'm alone with Bea again, when the doctors come in to check her condition against the new medication after yesterday's examination. With the good news that it's starting to work, they've asked me to wait in the hall or go down to the cafeteria for food.

For the next hour, I'm in the back corner of the cafeteria diving deep into my work, knowing, if nothing else, it's the most secure future I have and I need something to focus on.

Heartbreak is real. I know it's only been one magical night. But sometimes that's all it takes to know.

With everything these last couple of days have brought to the surface, I shouldn't be feeling like seeing my parents, but they're just across the city in the nursing home.

Making the decision, I tell the people at the nurses' station what's happening and to call me if things change.

Jumping in Misty, I'm across the city readying myself to

be two different people to the two people who are supposed to always be in my corner.

The lady at the front desk takes my ID and smiles, "Welcome Marcus, your parents are in the recreation room."

I hide my surprise that they're in the same room and make my way through the security doors and into the masses of bodies in the various stages and ages of health.

I see Ma first in her wheelchair, over by the window, looking more frail than the last time I was here.

Approaching, I tentatively say, "Hey Peggy. How are you today?"

Her gaze leaves the beautiful gardens outside and travels to me. "Danny, you look different. Don't we have a game today?"

I guess that answers my question. I have to be Danny the outfielder on her softball team. When I discovered I had to be this character I had to research not only the position, but the man as well.

"It's not until later. Do you want to go outside?"

"Good luck with that. These vile people won't let me out. No matter how much I beg."

That sounds like the old Ma I remember. A firecracker, ever protective and determined.

"Yeah, I get that. But I have power." I waggle my eyebrows. "Let's go."

Gazing around at the other occupants, I can't see Dad. I'll just have to find him before I leave.

I push through the doors and the moment the warm sun and fresh air hits her face, there's an audible sigh of relief from both of us.

Making our way over to a bench, I sit down. Just being in her presence is calming me. This is what I needed. She may not know who I am, but I can show her how much I love just being in her company.

We're quite a sight, both of us have our face turned to the afternoon sun, eyes closed and watching memories of days or years past.

I've no idea how long we stay like this, my foot resting on Ma's light enough that I can feel her flinch. But 'Danny' wasn't intimate with her, so this is the only touching I can get away with.

"Son?" A voice breaks though my memories, but I haven't heard it in nearly two years as clear as just now. I'm not sure if it is a memory, so I'm still sitting as I was.

"Marcus Cameron O'Brien, open your damn eyes." That's the stern loving voice I remember from my childhood as my Dad would chastise me for doing something stupid.

Snapping my eyes open, I'm locking them with the same brown eyes as mine.

"Peggy." His voice is softer, perhaps he knows that he doesn't know which version he'll get. His condition wasn't as severe as hers in the beginning, but still bad enough he couldn't be left alone or near her. In her violent incidences, Ma is the savage pitcher she was in her youth.

"Jeff." Looking to me and blinking a few times, like she's clearing her eyes, "Marcus?"

I can't control my actions, I'm up and wrapping my arms around both of them. Whatever miracle has happened to give me this one precious moment, I'll take it.

The nurse behind Dad's wheelchair says, "I'll just be over there." She indicates with her head. "You may not have long, soak it up."

"Son, tell us everything."

Starting with my return from Europe all the way to Bea in the hospital, I fill them in on the last six months of my life. All the while, they're holding hands like the life-long lovers they were before an invisible illness took them from me.

"I'm glad you got Misty." My dad is rubbing his hands over Ma's. "Your dreams are as important as your reality. Don't forget that."

"What will you do about Lexi?" Ma asks in her sweet motherly tone, not the harsh pitcher or across the fence fighter with dad.

"What can I do? She can't leave town and I'm a free spirit. She hasn't been in contact since the first day I was with Bea. Perhaps it's over before it even started. People have one night stands all the time. It's her way, anyway. She told me so."

Ma's brow is starting to crinkle, I think I'm losing her and I'm not ready to. Dad sees it as well.

"Go to her son. Tell her everything. Bea is fine and you're not a doctor. Live."

"Jeff. Get back to your yard." Ma's tone is harsh again. I've lost her.

Waving the nurse over, she knows what to do.

"Peggy." His voice is soft as he realises she's back being the feisty teenager again.

I'm raising to move behind Ma's chair and I grab her handles to take her back inside as I watch the nurse move away with Dad, further into the garden.

"Danny, I swear. That man has been my pain and saviour my whole life. If he wasn't the son of my parents archnemeses, I'd marry him."

"I know Peggy. I know."

Heading back to the hospital, the sun is setting behind me. I've decided one more night. I'll endure the hospital for one more night and use this time to reflect and really think about what I want.

Nodding to the staff at the nurse's station, I'm entering Bea's room and the first thing that hits me is the silence. I left to the sound of machines and her life.

Racing to her side, I'm about to press the call button when I feel the warmth in her skin and see her life raising and falling from her chest.

Sighing in relief, I slump in the chair, holding her hand.

"They remembered, Bea. I left you for a bit and went to my parents. And they were Ma and Dad for the first time together in what feels like forever. For that small amount of time I felt so free." Lowering my head, I add, "I'm going back to Lexi. I can't wait to find out what she wants. I have to find out."

A hand rests on my shoulder and I should jump at the contact, but I'm strung out. I've got nothing left. Just give me peace.

"Baby, I'm here."

No, she's not. Lexi wouldn't be here. This isn't a seaside village with my print shop, her gym and no pain.

With another squeeze to my shoulder, the voice that sounds like Lexi's whispers, "Marcus, I'm here. You don't have to find out. I'm here."

That *is* her. Raising my head and turning, I find Lexi behind me and Maggie at the end of Bea's bed.

"But how? How are you here?" I throw my arms around her waist. This is my missing piece, and I don't care about the stigma. Grown men are allowed to cry.

She taps my back and I loosen my hold, but I can't let her go. Pulling away she says, "I'm sorry it took us this long to get here, but I had to concentrate. That's why my phone was off."

Raising from the chair beside Bea's bed, her smile is watery and she moves her hands to hold my shirt like it's a lifeline. She can do whatever she needs to stay grounded to me.

"We discovered driving at night was the easiest.' Maggie adds with a look of awe in her eyes. "We arrived last night, but Lexi was too strained to come today. We had to wait until evening."

"I still can't believe you're here. Both of you." I turn to Maggie. "Thank you." She nods and excuses herself, then leaves the room.

Sitting back down, I put Lexi in my lap and hold her. This day has been an emotional roller coaster that has me leaning into her.

Gathering her even closer, I turn her face towards mine. "You're mine." I kiss her like it's the first, last and eternity all wrapped up in one.

CHAPTER 13
LEXI

Sitting on Marcus' lap, I soak up his presence. He is the only person to give me the strength and courage to face my fear and leave my town.

Breaking from our kiss. All I can see is my future as I look deeply into his beautiful brown eyes. "I'm yours."

We sit in silence looking at Bea, not knowing what will happen. The skin that can be seen around her hospital gown has a variety of bruises and colours from the accident.

This larger-than-life woman has been left fighting for her life because of me. No matter what anyone says, she was going to see Alfie for me.

The information he passed onto Maggie added to the details about his fraud issues.

Snuggling deeper into Marcus because I can, and just being here, I've never felt this safe or wanted. And it sinks in. This is the one.

Sitting up, I'm facing Marcus so fast his face has a stunned look of happiness. "Marry me?"

Of course there's shock on his face, but my smile softens his features. "What?"

"You heard me. Mags can do it. Let's do it here. Bea's here for you. I'll go and get Mags."

Jumping off his lap, I'm out the door looking for Maggie before he can even give me an answer.

"Mags." I find her talking at the desk with the staff. As I grab a stem of leaves from the bouquet on the desk, I'm weaving and twisting it into two rings while saying. "I need you to marry Marcus and I."

Finishing the pair of rings, I look into her face. I know this is the craziest, happiest, most outrageous thing I could've ever suggested. It's reflected in her eyes.

"I haven't seen you like this since before your parents died. There's been some snippets, but right now, there's pure love and life." She hugs me like only a best friend can. "Of course."

Making our way back to Marcus, he's still sitting there holding Bea's hand. But he's not looking dejected and beaten like he was before.

Hearing us come in, Maggie steps up and says her piece. "I'll perform the ceremony, but it won't be legal as such. I'm only doing this because no one, not even me has brought her this much happiness." She indicates to me. "So, let's get you two married."

Maggie moves to one side of Bea's bed, with Marcus and I on the other. Holding hands, we're both grounding each other.

"I stand before you both as a friend of Lexi who is willing to let her go because I know that you, Marcus will love and cherish her 'til your final breath and beyond. Although it's short notice, but Marcus is there anything you'd like to say?"

"Lexi, sweetheart, I still can't believe that you're here with me. I was coming back. I can't live without you. These last few days have been the hardest in my life. But today my parents showed me that love, no matter the pain, is worth it. And you're so fucking worth it."

I can't help it. He's getting blurry from the water works collecting in my eyes. I close the gap quickly and kiss him on the cheek. After all, I need to keep this semi-professional. Otherwise, we'd be lip locked for the next little while.

"Now Lex, is there anything you'd like to say to Marcus?"

I have the rest of my life to share all of my stories, problems and achievements with him. But right now I only need to say one thing. "From the moment I locked eyes with you at the pub I knew you had more strength than any eye of a storm. Marcus, I love how you make me feel and I know that we'll be forever, because…" I lower my head, taking a deep breath, then raise my eyes to look into his. "I'm yours. I want you. And it will only ever be you."

I hear Maggie sniff. She truly knows the weight and meaning behind every one of those words.

Marcus' eyes are shimmering with as many emotions as I feel my own are telling him.

Feeling like we're in our own little bubble and truly thankful for this to be our wedding, I reach into my pocket and remove the two naturally woven rings I made out at the nurse's station and hold onto Marcus' hand. "I didn't have the time to buy you a ring and I doubt you have one for me, but it wouldn't be a wedding without a ring."

Sliding the ring onto his finger, it doesn't quite fit. With a little bit of wiggling, we know it won't fall off in the meantime and the smile on his face says that it's perfect in every way.

As he slides the makeshift ring onto my finger, I doubt I will ever take this off.

Maggie clears her throat. The emotion in the room seems to be getting to the woman who normally has them bottled up tight. "As the witness to this union I now pronounce you man and wife. You may kiss."

Every part of this moment is perfect. Our kiss is no different. Most wedding kisses are the normal lips locking in happiness. Not ours. Marcus is holding my face, like he won't ever let me go and I'm trying to balance my nerves and excitement at becoming his wife with my hands on his hips. He licks across my bottom lip wanting entrance, except if I open, I know it will not stay hospital friendly. Holding on to each other for support we finally pull apart to rest our foreheads together and just be present in our love for one another.

A hoarse voice breaks the silence in the room. "Thank fuck."

All eyes fly to Bea, who's lying there with a smile on her face letting us know she's been with us this whole time.

CHAPTER 14
MARCUS

It's been two weeks since my fake marriage to Lexi and there's nothing fake about it. Every night I'm in her bed and every morning neither of us leave the house without an orgasm. Even with only stars in the sky, when Lexi is getting ready for her Sparrow classes, I always find time to ensure she's leaving with a smile on her face.

Bea was released a week ago and between all of us and Alfie, she's getting a well balance of aftercare and recovery. She wasn't super excited to be seeing Alfie until I busted her arse and explained his reaction and concern while she was in a coma.

Maggie has summoned Lexi to her office today to explain the situation with Garry and there's nowhere else I'd want to be. She is my wife in all areas that matter, and I will protect her as best as I can.

It seems once Bea came out of her coma, Garry disappeared. The whole time, Lexi has been looking over her shoulder and I won't have that for someone I love. Especially not my wife.

Welcoming us, Maggie closes the door behind us before

sitting behind her large mahogany desk. We're in the comfortable leather chairs on the other side of the desk.

"Firstly, let me say, married life looks good on you two. But if you want it to be legal, the least you can do is book a time with a judge."

Taking Lexi's hand I say, "Thanks Maggie, we'll think about it."

Lexi gives my hand a squeeze and starts. "So, what's happening with Garry?"

Maggie's smile looks like one of victory. "I love that you're always direct. I may as well let you know. Garry is in custody. He was found last night, two states away. He's being transported back for trial. At this stage, a statement will be sufficient evidence."

The weight that this is finally over falls off her shoulders. It's like she can take her first full breath since I met her.

"Mags, so it's done? I just have to give the statement about him sending in that actor and his desire to take my business away from me? There won't be anything else?"

I admire my wife even more. Her strength continues to grow and shine.

"Yep, that's pretty much it. You may be asked as a witness at the trial, but I will be working against that." Her smile is adoration at her best friend. "You two are free to live your life looking forward. Garry Cawbourne can't reach you. I'll see you later." Standing up, she comes up and around her desk to hug us both.

She whispers something in Lexi's ear, then we're out and climbing in Misty. "Do I need to know what Maggie whispered to you?"

Her smile is even more radiating than it was this morning. The news has truly lifted all shadows from her eyes. "You're a keeper. That's all she said. Just telling me, what I already knew."

Fuck I love this woman. Heading to Fitness Freaks, I drop her off with a kiss before heading to my shop.

It's hard to believe that less than a month ago, I was new to this town, only here because Bea lived here. Now, there's nowhere else I'd want to be. I have my dream shop, dream woman and life is falling where it needs to be.

EPILOGUE
LEXI

3 Years later

Packing my car, I can't believe I'm leaving the country. Fuck, I'm amazed I can even leave the town by myself. And it's all because of my marvellous husband.

I know if he had not waltzed into this town, dragged here by Bea and especially to the bar that Friday night, I would still be confined to the town's limits.

Watching him lock up our house, his actions are meticulous like his amazing printing and graphic design business. In the last three years it's grown so much that he has a trainee on and can spend more time with me.

He also gave me the courage and understanding to expand my gym. Because I was able to leave the town, I ventured out to speak and see how other gyms were running. In the last two years, I've expanded to twenty-four-hour access and I've been able to employ another trainer who helps with classes. We also have nutrition talks, women's health seminars and themed days. On top of that with the new changes I needed an administrative person, and who better than Bea. It's an added bonus that Alfie is still on the scene keeping her well-grounded.

Maggie continues to be the town solicitor and since word got out about Garry she was well sought after. He was sentenced to twenty years in jail, with no parole for sixteen years. Her relationship with Buck started as a professional one, yet I knew it wouldn't take long for them to realise they are perfect for each other. They join Bea and Alfie at our place for Sunday barbeques quite frequently.

This overseas trip is sort of an anniversary one for us. We've learned to live to our highest levels.

Marcus lost his parents last year. A sadness that I knew, but I still couldn't comprehend his pain. All I could do was be there with him through it all. I'd been lucky enough to meet Peggy and Jeff. To Peggy and Jeff, I was someone from high school who worked as a waitress at a diner they'd both frequented with their softball teams. It was beautifully sad to see their pain. On an occasion we were there, and they were Peggy and Jeff— Marcus' parents— I saw love and pain mixed together in every breath. They'd died peacefully in their sleep two nights apart. Jeff was first and Peggy was inconsolable for two days. All she wanted was Jeff and that broke Marcus the most.

"What are you thinking about sweetheart, you okay?"

Marcus' voice has so much power, it always centres me and brings me back to the present. It has helped in so many ways. Giving me the power to leave our town by myself and just now, bringing me back to appreciate the man in front of me.

"I'm definitely good. I was just thinking about the last three years. How I met you and everything that happened after that point." Leaning in to lightly kiss his lips I wrap my arms around his neck. "And yes, I'm okay. I'm a little nervous, but in a good way"

Kissing him hard on the lips and running my tongue along the seam of his mouth he opens to give me access. I moan when his tongue contacts mine and his hands cup my ass. I have to pull away.

"Fuck, Marcus if we don't stop now, we'll be late for our flight."

I'd be lying if we hadn't learnt that the hard way. A flight to the east coast had become more memories than just the sights.

Laughing and lowering me back to the ground, he gives me a light peck on the lips. "Sorry gorgeous, it's hard to stop once I have you within inches of my body."

Highlighting 'hard' by rubbing his semi against my stomach, it doesn't take much these days. I'm sure if I hadn't pulled away he'd have me on the bonnet out here in the driveway.

Putting more distance between us, but never dropping my smile, I round my car to the passenger's side. Marcus chuckles and gets in, starting our journey to the airport for our next adventure, with his hand on my thigh the whole way. We aren't taking Misty because I won't let her sit in airport parking for two weeks. She's still a classic and needs proper security at home.

The drive is filled with memories, dreams and ideas for our trip through Italy. All we'd planned was the departure flight, two nights accommodation and a departure date.

We could afford business or first class, but Marcus had decided to keep us in 'normal' class. He'd told me that once we made that leap into the other section we would never go back. And with many adventures planned for our future, we had to refrain from the luxury— at least at this stage.

Grabbing my hand, letting me know he'll always be there for me, I know I will never take his man for granted. Sure, I'd prefer a private plane like what I've read about, but that isn't our life.

Getting through security and boarding the plane, Marcus is leaning on my shoulder in our seats, giving me feather kisses along my neck. "I've got you. Forever and always." His kisses are relaxing my anxiety. The takeoff and landing are the most stressful. Gods, I hope they have some good entertainment to take my mind from the throbbing starting in my core because I'm in close proximity to my husband. No one on the plane needs to know about my dirty thoughts.

We managed to only kiss here and there throughout the flight to Rome. That wasn't the case when we finally made it to the hotel room. We might have gone cheap on the flights, but I soon learnt that my husband likes his luxuries. Hotel rooms are rarely below four stars. I never complain, because as soon as that door is closed, his strong arms band around me and he picks me up. My legs instantly wrap around his waist. They know what to do. It's pure instinct.

Kissing my neck, giving little licks and small bites, my moans can't be contained. "I see those gym sessions are paying off."

Running my fingers across the expanse of muscles across his shoulders, I am thankful I've been training him. I know it's a woman's only gym and we've nearly been caught using the twenty-hour access, but he's the only man in the gym and most of the time, it's a set time and a personalised program. I couldn't be without my husband.

"I've had the best trainer."

I feel the moment his legs hit the bed, I have no idea what the suite looks like, I only have eyes for him. The mattress meets my back and Marcus follows me down. I can certainly appreciate the softness of the comforter that begins to swallow us.

"I've got the best husband."

We never actually changed our vows from when Maggie did them in Bea's hospital room. Our rings have been upgraded to simple bands with a vine design to match the ones I made that day. But it's all we need. In all the eyes that matter, we are husband and wife.

Making quick work of our clothes, we lay gazing into each other's eyes. His hard cock rubs up and down my slit gathering moisture. Both of us getting more worked up with every stroke through my pussy lips. It's moments like this that bring everything together. "I love you Marcus. You truly are my world, and I want everything with you."

It didn't need to be sealed with a kiss, it just needed to be said. "Sexy Lexi, you are my everything. My love, my life, my heart, my soul, my forever and always. I love you."

With his declaration, he pushes in and locks our souls together. We've made love many times before. We've fucked on every surface in our house, and every hotel we've been in. Every time feels like the first time. The magic has never left us and there's no sign of it dying out.

ACKNOWLEDGMENTS
WITH THANKS

Let me tell you readers, this was one of those books that took everything and then some from start to finish. It was never 'easy' to write, the story didn't just flow like The Assistant and The Apprentice. However, it got here into your hot little hands with the help of friends we've got the final product. Some friends gave me the character names, with a quick thought and a passing comment, we had Sexy Lexi and Marcus. Other friends gave me the idea as to who the villain was. Or there were the friends at the gym giving me ideas as to what workout could go in this story. Please let me know how far you go in the workout Lexi gave Marcus. In thirty minutes, I was only able to complete the 20 reps and the 15 reps cycle. Plus, other friends were all there on the sideline filled with encouragement to get this strong woman's story out.

It is also with thanks that I acknowledge my professional team. What an adventure this little beauty led us on. But she is here now.

And as always, thank you readers. If you've made it this far and got through it all, I appreciate you. I hope my little palette cleansers of books are giving you just a little break from reality and you're enjoying a little time to yourselves.

Stay passionate and thank you.

— Tess Molesworth xxoo

ABOUT THE AUTHOR

Tess Molesworth grew up in a small country town in NSW, and now lives not far from there.

A lover of life, writing and spending time with close friends, Tess' superpower is her infectious laughter that leaves you wanting more.

Tess is a compassionate and ardent dreamer who is always willing to tell you a story, and can be found crafting them in her favourite local pub.

ALSO BY TESS MOLESWORTH

BOOK 1 - The Assistant

https://tessmolesworth.com/shop/p/the-assistant-by-tess-molesworth

BOOK 2 - The Apprentice

https://tessmolesworth.com/shop/p/the-assistant-by-tess-molesworth-2btzd

BOOK 2.5 - The Hacker

https://tessmolesworth.com/shop/p/the-assistant-by-tess-molesworth-2btzd-3w89d-59nnf

BOOK 3 - The Designer

https://tessmolesworth.com/shop/p/the-assistant-by-tess-molesworth-2btzd-3w89d

www.ingramcontent.com/pod-product-compliance
Lightning Source LLC
LaVergne TN
LVHW091933070526
838200LV00068B/955